He's Mine

A Romance Novel

A T.S. Connor Book

Published by T.S. Connor Publishing INC.

A division of CreateSpace

Charleston, SC

ISBN-13: 978-0997968804

To my Princess

Kenzie,

Thanks for being the

bundle of joy that lights up

my life.

Acknowledgements

I would first like to thank my Heavenly Father for blessing me with a great imagination and the ability to tell a story.

I want to thank everyone that assisted me in this journey of completing this entire project. Special thanks to my editor Valarie D. for helping me perfect my craft, my graphic designer Devise for bringing my cover and back of the book to life, to my sisters Asia and Quaniqua for listening and giving me feedback, and my barber Damon “DJ The Barber” for being my male model for the cover. Finally, special thanks to my mother for being a great role model and shaping me into the woman that I’ve become.

Prologue:

Then

"Damn girl, you still lying in bed? You do know it's late in the afternoon, right? Come on now get up! TJ called and told me to get you up and out of the house today so no more drowning in depression. I know you hear me Kelsey."

Kendra whined as she pulled the covers back and nudged me to get out of the bed. I looked a hot mess and I'm pretty sure my room matched my appearance. I had on the same dingy white t-shirt and pajama pants for the third day in a row now and my hair was matted in disarray but with my current frame of mind, appearance and hygiene was the least of my concerns.

"Leave me alone and let me drown in my depression. Life is better if I don't have to deal with it," I complained.

“You have so much to live for Kels. What about your son, your successful career, and your family?” Kendra was trying to be the sunlight in the midst of a thunderstorm but I still couldn't see the light at the end of this gloomy tunnel.

“My family was ripped away from me the night my husband was killed. Now for the last time leave me alone Kendra!” I snatched the sheets back from her and covered my head with no hesitation. I wanted her to leave. I wanted to sulk in solitude. I actually wanted to die.

“Fine, I’ll leave you alone for now but I’ll still be here cleaning up this messy house.” She stared at me with pleading eyes as if she wanted to further probe me but she understood that my current emotions were beyond earth shattering.

Kendra gently shut the door behind her and finally left my bedroom which had been so empty and cold ever since the night of my wedding anniversary. That was the day that drastically changed my life forever. It was the night that my husband, my best friend, was killed in a fatal car accident by a drunk driver. Tristan and I had been together since we were sixteen years old. We were engaged at 22 and married by the time we turned 24. We also had a handsome son together. My husband was definitely more of a man that any woman could ever ask for. I'm still in denial about his death and the fact that eventually I will have to snap back into reality. However, it's only been a few months since his funeral and my wounds still feel as open as they did the night I was informed of his death.

The last night we shared together was special. We were celebrating our eight year anniversary. We ran out of wine after we made love so he decided to run to the store to get some more. While he was doing that I decided to make the scene more romantic. I put on some slow music, dimmed the lights and lit some candles and put on some sexy black lace lingerie. Instead of seeing his handsome face again I was startled with a phone call telling me that my husband had been a victim of a tragic car accident. My life hasn't been the same since. My husband was all I knew.

I got out of the bed for the first time in three days. I hadn't eaten in three days, showered, or spent any time with my son. Not to mention that I had gained over thirty pounds since Tristan's funeral. Food was definitely my way of comforting myself. I don't know what came over me when I finally crawled out of bed without anyone's encouragement. I stopped when I passed the mirror in my bedroom and stared at my reflection. I was ashamed to look at myself. I had never been the type of woman to just let herself go even after marriage and pregnancy. I finally realized that I still had a life and a son to live for. It was time for me to start living again.

Chapter One:

Now

"Man that was a good workout. Look at you girl, you've lost all of that weight you had gained."

"Thanks, I've been working out five days a week and eating healthy. It's been paying off thanks to your health tips. They actually work", I said as I wiped the sweat from my forehead.

"Well you know it's what I went to college for girl. I know what I'm doing!" said Kendra.

Kendra and I have been best friends since the day we met in third grade. She was always the pretty dark skinned girl with a sassy attitude to match. She had beautiful long thick hair that went beyond her bra strap and slanted almond-shaped eyes with high cheekbones. My girl was gorgeous. Most people wonder why we're best friends because she's so outgoing and I'm more reserved. I guess we've always balanced each other out. She's a lot more than just a friend. Since we were both an only child, we naturally became more like sisters. She's definitely the best sister I could ask for. We went to middle school and high school together and of course we were roommates in college.

"So do you have any plans for tonight?" Kendra asked as we wiped down the treadmills we used and headed to the ladies locker room.

"You know it's basketball season and Tristan's basketball game is tonight at seven. It's pretty important. He has college scouts coming to see him. You know I wouldn't miss that for the world. You want to go with me?"

"Love to but I can't. I have another workout with one of my male friends if you know what I mean! Tell my nephew to have a good game and I'll definitely make the next one." Kendra claimed as she stripped down to her birthday suit to hop in the shower.

"Have I ever met your so called male friend or is this a new one?" I asked with questioning eyes.

"Don't worry about my male friends. You should be worried about clearing out some of those cobwebs from decorating your vagina. Show mini me some love for a change because you definitely need it!" Kendra yelled from the shower stall.

"Wow! Did you really just air my business out in front of all of these chicks in here? You definitely don't know what a filter is. Call me later so I can tell you how the game goes", I said to her through clenched teeth as she quickly dressed for her "workout".

"Will do, I'll talk to you later." She smiled from ear to ear as she grabbed her purse and car keys.

After Kendra left I decided to stay at the gym and relax in the sauna. I mean it wasn't like I had a boyfriend to rush home to. It was a great way for me to relax my muscles after a tense workout and meditate. I can't believe my son is a senior in high school now which means I am definitely getting old. I raised a respectful son with his head on straight. He maintains a 3.5 grade point average, is the star captain of his high school basketball team, and he was still holding on to his virginity. He certainly reminds me of his father when were in high school.

After showering at the gym and changing back into my sundress and putting my hair into a neat bun, I headed to my son's school to see him play. I was seated comfortably in my all black Infinity truck and enjoying my R&B 90's playlist. I waited for the light to change to green when all of a sudden I was rear ended into the intersection and nearly hit by oncoming cars. The sound of metal clashing and glass shattering terrified me but I felt blessed because I didn't have any major injuries due to me *always* wearing my seat belt. I couldn't wait to meet the idiot who obviously didn't know how to drive. As I was unbuckling my seat belt, I heard a knock on the window. He looked very familiar yet I couldn't remember where I knew his face from. Despite being so frantic, he was fine as hell.

"Oh my God! Are you okay?" The man asked me as I stumbled out of my truck.

"I'm fine. You seem to be okay. You didn't see me stopped at the red light?" I desperately tried to be angry with him but his concern for my safety on top of his good looks quickly put a stop to my attitude.

"I'm sorry. I was distracted arguing with my fiancée on the phone. Don't worry about the damages. I'll cover everything. Here is my card with my information." He handed me his business card then rubbed his hand over the waves in his hair.

The police arrived on the scene and confirmed that the accident wasn't my fault. They took pictures and conducted their investigation. As I waited for a cab, my son called me asking why I wasn't at the game yet. I told him what happened and ensured him that I was okay. My cab was taking forever to pick me up so the familiar looking stranger approached me once again.

“I am really sorry about this. Do you need anything? I feel horrible”, he explained as he stuck his massive hands in his dress pants pockets. Distracted by his movements, my attention immediately dropped to his crotch area. I quickly diverted my gaze back to his pretty brown eyes before he noticed just how far my mind had drifted into the gutter.

“No, it’s fine. I’m just waiting on my cab.” I stood with my arms folded across my chest. His presence was making me nervous.

“Well, if you do need a ride I can take you wherever you need to go. My rental will be here pretty soon. The next cab will probably be thirty minutes to an hour in this traffic. It’s the least I can do.” He smiled and his pearly whites made me melt inside.

“I don’t get in cars with strangers.” I was very hesitant but I definitely couldn’t miss my son’s game.

“If I’m not mistaken I think we went to college together. Your name is Kelsey, right? Your best friend’s name was Kendra if I remember correctly. I couldn't forget Kendra's vivacious personality even if I tried. You don't remember me?" He asked as he flashed those pearly white teeth again.

I knew he looked familiar! How could I forget his face? I had a huge crush on him in college even when my late husband and I were dating. I met him on freshman move in day. Not only was he handsome but he had a great personality and a sense of respect for women that most guys in our age definitely didn't have. He showed interest in me as well but he also respected the fact that I was in a relationship. Yeah, I remember him very well now.

"Wow, Demetri? Yeah, I remember you now. It's been years since I've seen you. How is your mom doing?"

"Her health isn't in its best state right now. I just moved back some months ago to take care of her."

"Oh, that's sad to hear, I hope she gets well soon. I'll take the ride though. I need to get to my son's game."

"Okay, cool my rental just pulled up." Demetri escorted me to his Range Rover.

I was no longer uncomfortable sitting next to him like I had been before which is rather strange considering that I hadn't felt comfortable around other men at all since my late husband's death. I definitely hadn't been intimate with another man since Tristan died let alone casually date. We reminisced about some old college memories as I secretly gave him a quick head to toe glance while his attention was focused on the road. He looked pretty much the same since college. He always kept a low haircut and clean face which is actually my preference. However, he did put on a lot of muscles since college though. He stood at six foot three, caramel complexion with succulent lips and of course I couldn't stop staring at his pretty light brown eyes. This man was still fine. He suddenly woke me up from my daydream when he spoke.

"How old is your son?"

"He'll be eighteen years old soon. He's doing well in school and he'll be going to college in a few months."

"That's good we need more educated well-mannered black men in society. How's your husband? It's Tristian, right?"

"Yeah, my husband was killed in a car accident some years back." I said as I looked down at my finger that used to be decorated with my wedding ring. It was a habit that I still had.

"I'm so sorry. I didn't know. I'm just going to put my foot in my mouth now."

"It's okay. I've dealt with his death. It was hard but I've accepted what happened."

"Okay, but on a lighter note, did you do anything with your psychology degree?"

"I became a clinical psychologist. I went back to school for my doctorate degree after Tristian's death. Now I own my own practice. I'm doing well so I can't complain. How about you? What did you get into after college?"

"I followed my father's footsteps and became a defense attorney. My father and I are partners at our firm. I'm pretty well off myself. The only thing I really want out of life now is to have children. I never had that luxury."

I noticed that his facial expression tensed as he said this. His jawline clinched while he kept his eyes on the road. His occupation now explained why he was wearing a three piece suit in this hot weather, I thought to myself.

"There's nothing like seeing your child grow from a fetus to a human being. It's a blessing that some people take for granted." I tried to use my words carefully since I noticed the topic of not having any children obviously bothered him.

“I definitely agree with you.”

When we finally made it to my son’s high school I almost didn’t want to get out of the car. I knew it was the fourth quarter because it was almost 9.00 p.m. I thanked Demetri for the ride and as I was about to close the door he asked for my number. I readily agreed and gave him my cell phone number. I felt as if someone was staring at me as I strolled to the double doors of TJ’s school. I turned around and seen that his eyes were glued on me and he didn't try to hide the fact that he just got caught mentally undressing me. My ass was definitely hurting from Kendra forcing me to do those squats today, but thank God she did because I know it was looking lovely in my green halter top sundress.

As usual my son had a great game. We went to eat at *AppleBee’s* restaurant after his game before heading home in the car I had bought him when he turned sixteen. I couldn’t wait to tell Kendra about the blast from the past I had today. I picked up my house phone and waited for her to answer.

“Hello”, said Kendra.

“So how was your little friend?” I was anxious to know since my sex life was nonexistent.

“Girl exactly what you just said. He was very little and disappointing. He didn't know what the hell he was doing so I left him hanging high and dry. You know me. How was the game though?”

“I missed majority of the game but from his stats it was good. So guess who ran into me today, literally?”

“Who and what do you mean literally?”

“I was at a red light and this car rear ended me. Turns out it was an old friend from college. Do you remember Demetri Latimore?”

“Yeah, I remember you used to have a huge crush on him. I remember his fine ass friend too. Did y’all talk”?

“Yeah we caught up on the present and reminisced about the past. It felt like we picked up where we left off and I was surprised to actually find myself smiling so much.”

“Wow, I haven’t heard you this excited about a man since Tristan. Is he single?”

"I wish. He's engaged to be married. Maybe we weren't meant for each other because the timing is never right."

"You're talking like he's already married. Maybe he feels the same way you do. You never know."

"So when do you plan on settling down instead of having fun with these so called '"friends"'?"

"Look I have issues. I need a man who can handle me physically, emotionally and especially sexually. I need someone who's on my level or above my level and most men can't handle that."

"I know you don't wanna hear me preach on my soap box but remember every man isn't worthy of entering your temple. Treat the body you have with respect. You only get one."

"Okay, that's the end of this conversation. I really don't want to hear that. I'll see you tomorrow", Kendra snared as she clicked the phone in my ear.

This is typical Kendra. She never liked hearing the truth but she knew I was right. I got ready for bed since I needed to be up early for work tomorrow. I had a new patient whose file I'd already studied before meeting with her. This new patient had some serious issues based off of our phone consultation. I needed all the rest I could get in preparation for tomorrow.

The next morning I woke up early to have breakfast with my son. I made some oatmeal with bananas, a cheese omelet with bell peppers and two smoothies for us. My son came into the kitchen and kissed me on the forehead like he always does. My baby boy is all grown up now.

“How did you sleep?” I asked.

“I always sleep well after a good game. So, what’s up with your car?” He asked as he took a seat on the barstool posted by the island in our kitchen.

“It’s in the shop getting repaired. I have a rental for now.”

“Well, I’m glad you’re okay. When you told me you had an accident I had a flashback and panicked.” It's crazy how much he resembles his father. Even his forehead crinkles the same way his father’s used to whenever he was stressed.

“I know. I was shaken up for a bit too. Are you okay though?”

“Yeah I'm good now. I miss Pops though. He never got the chance to see me grow into a man.”

"That's not true. Trust me when I say he's watching down on you now. He's still in your heart wherever you go and he loved you so much. Don't ever forget that." I paused as I felt myself tearing up.

"I know. Thanks for breakfast, Ma. I got practice tonight so I'll see you later."

"Okay, let me know when you make it home if I'm not here. And drive safe!" I yelled at him as he grabbed his book bag and car keys and jetted for the back door.

"Alright, love you." He yelled in returned and slammed the door.

"Love you too", I said as if he could hear me.

My son and I have grown accustomed to showing affection to one another because you never know if it's the last time you'll ever see each other again. We never had a fight or an argument. My son has always been an obedient child since he was a little boy. His father made sure he knew the importance of respecting authority.

I made it to my office and checked my email as I rocked back and forth in my office chair. My new patient was due to show up any minute now. There was a knock at the door.

"Dr. Smith, your 8 o'clock appointment just arrived," my assistant informed me.

"Thanks, Tony. I'll be right there."

I walked down the hall to meet my new patient. When I entered the room I noticed that she was very well dressed and attractive. She actually resembled me with a darker complexion but it was clear that all that hair on her head was not hers, yet the resemblance was still quite strange.

"Good morning Miss Karma Watts. It's nice to finally meet you." I smiled as I took a seat across from her.

"Good morning, Dr. Smith. I've heard good things about your work." She smiled back.

"Thank you. So, I've already looked over your file. However, I would like for you to give me a bit more background information about yourself so that I can better assist you." I stated as I flipped to a blank page on my notepad to take notes.

"Sure. As you may already know I am a defense attorney. I have a successful career and even a great fiancé but I'm not happy with my life. I've been keeping some things from my fiancé that I think he should know but I just can't find the courage to tell him. These secrets that I've been holding in are definitely deal breakers if he were to ever find out."

"What exactly are these deal breakers that you speak of if you don't mind me asking?"

"When I was an undergraduate in college I was bit wild. I was out enjoying the college life when I ended up pregnant. After weighing my options I ultimately decided an abortion was the best option for me. Unfortunately, I got pregnant once again when I was in law school and had yet another abortion. Long story short is I am now unable to conceive and bear children due to the abortions. It's been driving me crazy because my fiancé has been hinting that he wants to start a family", she nervously explained as she chewed on her manicured fingernails.

"The best thing to do is to be honest with your fiancé. Starting off a marriage based on lies could only further create turbulence within the relationship and a guilty conscience for you. Do you think you can handle that conversation with your fiancé?" I inquired.

"I know I can't handle that conversation right now. My career is really starting to flourish and even if I could conceive children I wouldn't want a child right now. This might be selfish to say but for me it's not a loss. It gets worse though. My fiancé doesn't know that I have multiple personality disorder and that I am a paranoid schizophrenic. He just thinks my work is stressful and is causing me to have severe mood swings. I'm usually fine until I don't take my medication."

"I believe it is in your best interest to sit down with your fiancé and have this painful conversation with him as soon as possible." Her facial expression quickly changed from that of nervousness to anger.

"Thanks for your input doctor but it'll be a cold day in hell before I submit to doing that. We can definitely handle this damn situation on our own. Come on Karma! We don't need her fucking opinion anyway. I don't know why you came here in the first damn place", she yelled to herself as she grabbed her purse and stormed out of my office while slamming the door behind her.

"Okay, thanks for coming ladies", I mumbled to myself as I sat in my now empty office.

I had never seen multiple personality disorder up close and personal until that day. I was utterly shocked and surprised of how quick this young lady switched up on me. I'm still at a loss for words. I've never felt so blessed to be mentally healthy even after my husband's death.

My work day was finally over and it was almost time to meet Kendra for our daily workout which was well needed because this 8 o'clock appointment had raised my blood pressure. I needed to relieve some stress. I grabbed my workout gear and changed in my office before heading to the gym. Kendra was already there doing some cardio on the *StairMaster* machine.

“Girl, I had a stressful day at work today”, I shared with her as I started the machine next to hers.

“What happened? You had another bird fly over the coo coo’s nest?”

“I can’t say too much but multiple personality disorder. You know what I mean?”

“Say no more. I know exactly what you mean.”

Chapter Two:

Demetri

"Hey Ma, are you feeling better?" I asked as I took a seat next to her hospital bed.

"Yeah I'm getting the energy to do things on my own again. Where's your father? I thought he was coming too?"

"He's meeting with a client right now. He told me to tell you that he'll be here to spend the night with you."

"So, how's life treating you?"

"Everything is good, Ma."

She looked at me with concern in her eyes. Even though my Mama was well within her 60's she looked really good for her age and didn't have one wrinkle on her face. She usually takes care of her health but she's been stressed lately for some unknown reason because she refuses tell me.

“Plan on having any children anytime soon is what I meant? I want to have some grandchildren. Your father and I are only getting older”, she complained.

“I want kids just as much as you want grandchildren. We’re working on it. We have an appointment tomorrow morning to determine our chance of conceiving.”

“I want you to have kids but not with that woman you’re with now. I don’t like that girl! I told you that when you introduced us. My mother instincts tell me something is wrong with her. What happened to the young lady you went to college with? You used to be crazy about her. Now that girl I really liked.”

“Remember the accident I told you I had? She was the person I rear ended. She's doing well for herself too. She’s single now. Her husband was killed in a car accident years ago.”

“Wow, that’s sad to hear. Send her my condolences. You two should get reacquainted. Maybe that was meant to be.”

“Ma, I have to go. I’ll let you know how the appointment goes tomorrow.”

I gave my mama a kiss on the forehead and headed to my truck. I was used to hearing how my mama despised my fiancée with a passion. I couldn't help but think about her comments of Kelsey though. I was crazy about her in college and from the looks of it with this whole accident situation, I think I'm still crazy about her which would explain my excitement when she told me she was single. The timing for me to make her mine has never been right. I pulled up to the condo I shared with my fiancée expecting to meet her there but instead I was met with an empty nest. I picked up my phone and called her.

"Hello."

"Hey, I thought you were going to be home. Where are you?"

"I'm at the office. I have a big profile case that I'm preparing for", she said with attitude dripping from her tone.

"That's nice and all but I thought we were going to do the baby making tonight." I noticed that whenever she's ovulating she starts arguments on purpose to avoid any chance of intimacy. She thinks I'm stupid but I caught on to her antics a long time ago.

“The baby making is on pause. I have work to do Demetri.”

“Are you going to be able to make the appointment tomorrow?”

“We’ll see.”

“Bye. I’ll see you when I see you I guess.” My tolerance for her bullshit and attitude was wearing thin these days.

“Bye!” She yelled and hung up in my face.

I swear I feel like I’m in a relationship by myself sometimes. It was beautiful in the beginning. She was so passionate and so in love with me then all of a sudden she started changing for the worst. When I began to mention starting a family everything went downhill. Maybe my mother has been right these past two years.

Kelsey crossed my mind once again. I stared at my cell phone contemplating whether I should call her or not. She hasn’t changed a bit. She’s still intelligent and very sexy with the same caring personality and here I was sitting in a dark empty condo. I thought to myself why not call her? I waited for her to answer.

“Hello, Dr. Smith speaking.”

"Hey Kelsey this is Demetri. I was just calling to check on you." I don't know why but I was a little nervous to call you, I thought to myself.

"I'm fine I don't have any injuries. Are you okay?" She genuinely seemed concerned which I found very attractive. Karma didn't even bother asking me if I was okay after I told her about the car accident.

"Yeah I'm good. How's your car?"

"It should be out of the shop any day now. I have a rental until then."

"That's good. I was wondering if you wanted to grab a bite to eat this Friday."

"I'd love to but my son has a basketball game this Friday. You're welcomed to come if you'd like."

"That's fine too. I can use some entertainment in my life. I'll see on Friday."

"See you later."

Friday couldn't come soon enough. This would be my first time ever meeting her son. I hadn't talked to my guy for a few days now so I decided to call him. We usually talked every day but I had been so busy with work and trying to start a family that I forgot about my homie.

“What’s up Marcus? What you been up to?”

“Nothing major really. The usual, I just been working and kicking it with these females.”

“Man when you gone be a one woman man? You've been like that since middle school.”

“When I can find a woman that can satisfy my every need, one that don’t complain every five minutes or check my phone when I’m sleep”, Marcus laughed.

“So basically you want a woman with a male mentality?”

“Yes man that’s all I want! Is that too much to ask for?”

“Hell yeah! Most women don’t think and act like men bro. That’s rare, and if you do come across a woman like that she probably was a man and had her sex changed”, I joked with him.

“In that case I don’t want any parts of that bro. I’m good!”

“Hey guess who I ran into the other day?”

“Who did you run into?”

"Remember Kelsey from college? The girl that I been crazy about since I met her? I rear ended her talking to Karma's crazy ass on the phone."

"Yeah I remember her and her friend. I think her friend had a thing for me if I'm not mistaken. Her friend name was Kendra right? Yeah, I heard some things about her back in the day. From what I heard she wasn't shy in the bedroom bro. You got her number?"

"Why would I have Kendra's number? I have Kelsey's number though. I'm going to her son's game this Friday", I announced with huge a smile on my face.

"I thought she was married."

"She was. Her husband was killed in a car accident some years back. Mom's said I should talk to her instead of Karma. You know she can't stand Karma."

"To be honest bro I never liked her either but you a grown ass man. You can make your own decisions."

"How come you never told me that?"

"Because you were so infatuated with her and you seemed happy."

"Yeah, things have changed though. I'm not as happy as I once was and she doesn't even seem to care."

"If you not happy then what are you doing? You're about to marry this girl in less than a year!"

"I guess I was just settling because I couldn't have what I really wanted."

"I'm guessing you talking about Kelsey?"

"You guessed right."

"You got some thinking to do. We should go to the gym tomorrow. It's this gym I been trying to go to for a while now. They actually have a special going right now too."

"Yeah I'm down with that. Meet me there after 6 p.m."

"Okay, cool."

I headed to the new gym that Marcus was speaking of after work the next day. We met up in the parking lot and entered the gym. It was really nice inside. Besides the typical workout equipment there was a swimming pool area, a basketball and tennis court, and a steam room. This was my type of gym. There were a lot of women in here as well. Marcus was acting like a dog in heat when he seen all the women but I was cool as usual. Marcus noticed these two particular women doing squats on some type of high tech machine. They had their backs toward us and I couldn't help but enjoy the view.

"Bro, I know you see what I see. This might be my new work-out spot", said Marcus.

"I definitely see what you seeing right now."

"I got a soft spot for dark skinned women with long hair. I can't take my eyes off ole girl on the left. She needs to turn around so I can see her face." Marcus was making his gawking so obvious. He didn't even try to hide the fact that he was being super thirsty.

"Calm down bro don't seem too desperate. At least act like you came here to work out. Do some arm curls or something."

"Yeah, you right. Let me know when she turns around", he claimed as he sat down on a bench and picked up a 50 pound dumbbell.

"She's turning around now. That looks like Kendra!"

"That's her fine ass! I'm pretty sure that's Kelsey too. Man, Kendra's body is on point. I heard she was a personal trainer but damn. Fuck it, I'm about to go over there." Marcus immediately dropped the weight and walked over in Kendra's direction.

We all got reacquainted and chatted for a couple of hours at a restaurant near the gym. It felt like we were teenagers again without a care in the world. I can tell Kelsey was feeling me based off the way she acted towards me but she would never overstep her boundaries knowing that I'm engaged. As for Marcus, he was undeniably captivated with Kendra. I think he finally met his match. Kendra is certainly a challenge.

"So Marcus, what made you come to my gym?" asked Kendra.

"No reason in particular I just heard this was an upscale gym so I wanted to check it out."

"So what did you do with your major after we graduated?" asked Kendra.

"I became a forensic accountant for the police department", he boasted.

"Wow, I would have never guessed that you would have gone into that field", said Kendra.

"Why is that?"

"Because that career is more suited by nerds and I never got that vibe from you", said Kendra.

"Just because I have swag doesn't mean I'm not intelligent baby I can think with both heads if you know what I mean", Marcus smirked.

"I know exactly what you mean," said Kendra.

Kelsey and I decided to sit at the bar and leave Marcus and Kendra to flirt with each other. I don't even think they realized that we went to the bar because they were so enamored with one another. I was just happy to be in Kelsey's presence. I had a lot on my mind so our conversation immediately became deep.

"So how was your day?" asked Kelsey.

"Other than now it wasn't good whatsoever. My fiancée and I had a doctor's appointment today to determine our fertility but she didn't show up." I usually never share my inner thoughts with anyone but she made it so easy for me to open up to her.

"Does she want children?"

"I honestly don't know. I tell her that I want to start a family and she pushes me away. It's stressful", I explained with defeat as I circled my finger around the rim of my drink.

"Just let the situation play out. Maybe she feels pressured by you."

"Maybe but I don't want to wait until my forties to start a family either. I know you have Tristan but didn't you want a bigger family?"

"Yeah I always wanted more than one child because I am an only child so I knew how lonely it could be growing up but I only pictured having kids with the man I would marry. I would have loved to have more kids though. It just didn't work out that way."

"So, what if you fell in love again? Would you want to create another family?" I was subconsciously testing her and hoping her answers would be exactly what I was looking for relationship wise.

"If I were to fall in love again I would be open to it so most likely yeah I would have more kids. I would have to know for certain that he's the person I am in love with and the man for me though", she smiled.

"Yeah that's the only way to go. You like to do things the old fashioned way. I like that. I think that's why my mother really likes you. She asked about you by the way. She also wanted to send her condolences."

"Did she really? Tell her I said thanks. Your mom is hilarious. I missed being around her. Is your dad still a busy businessman?" She was winning brownie points with me for asking about my family and genuinely caring about what was going on with them. She just didn't know it. I'm very family oriented and I can tell she was the same way.

“Yeah he didn’t change one bit. He lives to be in the courtroom. You know I learned from the best”, I bragged.

“I’m sure you have. Are you still coming to the basketball game?”

“Yeah I can’t wait to see your son play. I see him on ESPN all the time. He’s definitely going to a good college with his skills and grades.” Kelsey and I were deep in conversation when Kendra and Marcus approached us at the bar.

“Kelsey don’t worry about giving me a ride home. Marcus is giving me a ride.”

“You sure that’s the only ride he’ll be giving you?” inquired Kelsey.

Marcus smirked at that question.

“Um, let me think about it? Probably not! Bye girl, I’ll talk to you later.”

“Bye Kendra.”

“Hey make sure you call me too,” I yelled to Marcus.

“Oh, I definitely will,” Marcus smiled.

After those two love birds left we chatted for another hour or so before Kelsey had to go home and get ready for work. Honestly, I didn’t want her to leave. She makes it so easy to be around her. I see why Tristan loved her the way he did. I felt myself dreading to go home to the woman I thought I was in love with while watching the woman I’ve always wanted walk away. I was determined to never let her walk away from me again. I knew what I had to do.

I noticed Karma finally made her way home when I made it back to our apartment. I rescheduled our doctor’s appointment for tomorrow morning and cancelled all of her morning appointments at work so she couldn’t wiggle her way out of this one. She was sleeping when I entered the room. I gathered my clothes and headed to bathroom. I stood in the shower and let the water run down my face and body. All I could think about was how unhappy I was right now and how satisfied I could be with Kelsey.

The next morning was normal as usual until she found out that I had cancelled her morning appointments. She went ballistic on me. I didn’t care though. I dragged her ass to that appointment and she cussed me out the entire way. She ignored me when we made it to her doctor's office. We anxiously waited in the room to hear what her doctor had to say about the tests and x-rays he performed on Karma. Suddenly, there was a knock at the door.

"Okay, I'm back with the test results and they don't look too promising Ms. Watts", her doctor claimed.

"What do you mean", I asked.

"Do you want him to leave the room Ms. Watts? This information is personal." I shot him a dirty look because he knew me well enough to know that I wasn't a stranger to her.

"No. He's going to be my husband soon. He can stay."

"Okay, well your chances of conceiving are very slim to none."

"Why is that? She's a perfectly healthy woman." I was sitting at the edge of my chair now because I was dying to know.

"As you can see here in this X-ray Karma's fallopian tubes are severely damaged", he said in a matter of fact tone.

"What can cause this damage? Can it be reversed?" I inquired.

"This damage can be caused by several things such as sexually transmitted diseases that go untreated for a long period of time or it can be caused by an abortion procedure that goes wrong. In Karma's case, two incorrectly performed abortion procedures have left her infertile."

I couldn't believe what I was hearing. So this is why she been standing me up on these appointments and avoiding the topic of children. She already knew she couldn't have kids. She's fucking selfish to lead me on for two years thinking we would have a family in the future. I was so angry that I stormed out of the doctor's office and left her ass there too. She can find her own way to work. She could walk there for all I cared.

I cancelled my meetings and went to visit my mother so I could vent and clear my mind. I already knew what my mother was going to say about Karma but I needed to hear the truth about her for myself. This little stunt she pulled today only pushed me farther away from her to the point where I felt like leaving her ass and being with Kelsey. I knocked on my mother's door.

"Come in Demetri. I know it's you."

"How did you know it was me?"

“Because I knew you and that girl had a fertility appointment today. What happened?” My mother questioned as she turned the volume down on the soap opera she was watching.

“Well long story short is she had two abortions that she never told me about and it left her unable to have children.”

“I hate to kick you while you’re down but I must say that I told you so. She’s not your spiritual soulmate I’ve stressed that to you a thousand times already. But what’s done in the dark *always* come to light and now you see her as the devious woman she’s always been.”

“I understand what you meant Ma but now I’ve seen it for myself.”

“So what happens now?”

“I think she gets the point that it’s over between us but if she doesn’t I’ll make it clear by putting her out and changing the locks. Besides, I’ve been hanging out with Kelsey lately and I’ve realized that the feelings I had for her in college have never gone away.” I smiled just at the thought of her.

“I saw a spark in your eyes when you first introduced us and I knew you really loved her then. I really did see her as my own daughter and I’ve always liked the way she carried herself as a woman. It's very sad what happened to her husband but my intuition tells me that this was meant to be for you two. I truly believe that she is your spiritual soulmate. You better snatch her up before somebody else does or you'll regret it for the rest of your life."

"I definitely won't let that happen again. Pops said he's taking you on a surprise date tonight after court since you're being released from the hospital today. He told me not to tell you so act surprised anyway. Get dressed and enjoy your date. I'll see you soon, Ma. I love you." I kissed her on her forehead and gathered my belongings.

"Okay, love you too and remember what I said."

I headed to my apartment to gather Karma's belongings and pack them up so they could be ready whenever she decided to come home. I had a locksmith coming out tomorrow morning to change the locks. I wanted this to be a peaceful separation but with her attitude I know that's not going to happen. I wish I could get back the two years that I had invested in our relationship. I'm returning that princess cut engagement ring that I bought and anything else I still have the receipt for. While I was packing Karma's shit I decided to call Marcus to see how his night cap went with Kendra. He answered on the fourth ring.

“What’s up bro? How was your night with Kendra?”

“She played me.”

“What happened?” I was itching to know.

“So during the entire ride home she was flirting with me, rubbing my dick and some more shit. I opened her car door for her when we made it to her place and walked her to her front door. I’m thinking she was going to invite me inside on some grown woman shit. Why did she tell me that I have to earn what she has to offer and slammed the door in my face? Left me to take a fucking cold shower that night. I was pissed!”

“On what! She played you like that? She must have changed since college because the old Kendra would have let you hit it. So what’s the next move?” I was being nosy.

“I’m taking her out Friday night and nigga mind your business!”

“Oh so it’s like that, huh? Nigga you feeling her even though she played you so just admit it”, I laughed at him.

"So what if I do like the girl? It ain't too many women that made me wait longer than the first night."

"Yeah, she'll give you a run for your money so you better be careful. I hear Karma coming in so I'll call you later."

"Alright, don't forget 'cause I want to hear all about yo night with Kelsey."

"It ain't nothing major to tell you but I will call you back."

"Okay."

Karma finally came inside and noticed I had packed her belongings. She wasn't too happy about that but I didn't care. She started with one of her temper tantrums.

"What the fuck is this Demetri? Why are you packing my shit?" She yelled as she threw her purse down on the sofa.

"Don't act stupid like you don't remember what happened at the doctor's office today. When were you going to tell me that you had two abortions and can't have kids?" I was trying to remain calm but it was becoming more and more difficult with her disrespect.

"When I felt like telling you is when I was going to tell you. It wasn't any of your damn business to know!"

"Are you fucking serious Karma? In that case you can take off that fucking ring I bought, give me the house keys and take yo shit I have packed for you. I don't want you near me. I no longer want any type of relationship with you. Do you understand me?"

"No! You are not leaving me that easy! I refuse to let you go to another bitch after I put all of my effort and hard work into this relationship. You got another thing coming if you thinking you gone ever leave me Demetri!"

Karma refused to leave my apartment. She started throwing my vases and breaking my flat screen TV's in my bedroom and living room. She even tried to slap me and put her hands on me. I was never raised to put my hands on a woman but she was really tempting me. I called the police in the midst of her attacking me and fucking up my apartment. The police came about 15 minutes later and arrested her. I did press charges and made a personal phone call to a judge who was a good friend of mine so that they could immediately place a restraining order on her to send her ass a message that we are clearly done. I was so glad I didn't marry her.

After she was taken into custody I tried to get my apartment back in order. I called Marcus back and told him everything that just occurred. He didn't seem too surprised. He simply told me he already knew she was a crazy bitch. Of course I called my parents and told them what happened. They told me I handled the situation well and to be careful. The last call I made was to Kelsey. I asked her to meet me so we could get something to eat and talk. She told me she'll be there in 20 minutes. I needed to be around someone who wouldn't stress me the fuck out. Besides, I missed her and wanted to see her.

We met at some random bar not too far from my apartment. She wasn't really dressed up at all. She was just leaving the gym. Although her long curly hair was pulled into a messy bun she still looked very attractive to me. I guess I looked stressed out because she ordered us a few rounds of shots to take off the edge.

"So, I'm guessing you had one hell of a day?" asked Kelsey.

"You don't know the half of it. I put a restraining order on my crazy ass EX fiancée. No man in his right mind could ever tolerate a woman like that. I've completely washed my hands of her."

"I'm glad to hear that. Since we're on the topic of your ex fiancée I should let you know that I have met her before", she said as she sipped her drink.

"Are you serious? How is that possible? She never mentioned you before."

"I'm bound by law so I can't say much other than she was very briefly one of my patients."

"Did she tell you anything I'm not aware of?"

"Come on Demetri you know I can't tell you that but trust me when I say you made the right decision by putting a restraining order on her."

"I guess I'll leave the topic of her alone then."

"Yeah, that's the best thing to do."

We were tipsy after a couple of drinks. Kelsey's favorite song came on so she sashayed her way to the dance floor. Our eyes locked as she swayed her hips from side to side while she moved eloquently and sexy all at the same time. I was getting excited watching her slow dance so I decided to join her. I walked up behind her and wrapped my arms around her small waist. She instantly draped her arms around my neck and grinded her ass on my groin. This exact moment reminded me of that party we went to our freshman year of college. She wasn't single at the time but that didn't hinder me from asking her to dance. She hesitated at first because she obviously didn't want to rock the boat in her relationship but she caved in eventually. She looked gorgeous as always that night. She didn't show a lot of skin but I had a good imagination. She was tall for a girl as is but she wore heels that night so she towered over me. Unfortunately, I hadn't quite reached my growth spurt yet but just like that night she had her arms around me caressing my neck. It was an upbeat song playing that night when she twerked on me despite the fact that someone might see us and tell her boyfriend. It was at the moment when I knew she had a thing for me. Just like that night in college I was so excited that my dick stood at attention and I'm pretty sure she feels it now like she felt it back then.

Once the song ended we went back to the bar hand in hand as I pulled her chair out for her. I took a seat and noticed the sultry look in her eyes. She looked as if she wanted to pounce on me. She took another sip of her drink and invited me back to her place for a night cap.

"You aren't driving are you?" I asked aware of the fact that we were both incapable of driving.

"No, I'll call a cab. It should be here any minute."

"So we're leaving our cars here?" I questioned.

“Yeah, I’ll have my son drop us off to our cars tomorrow.”

“Where is he if you don’t mind me asking?”

“He’s staying over at his teammate’s house for the night. They have an early practice.”

“That’s cool with me.” Little did she know that it was more than cool with me? I’d been fantasizing about this moment for years.

Chapter Three:

Kelsey

It was a little after eleven o'clock when we made it back to my place. It was a windy, cool night with a severe thunderstorm roaring outside. Demetri and I got caught in the midst of the rain on our way back to my house so I gave him some clothes to change in. We relaxed on my sofa in front of the fireplace to warm up. My legs were propped on his lap while we drank wine and talked about everything under the sun. Demetri started rubbing his hand up and down against my legs and for the first time in a long time my body responded to another man's touch. I felt a familiar sensation brewing inside of me that I remembered all too well. We stopped our conversation and glared into each other's eyes as if this moment was well overdue. He boldly leaned in towards me to give me a kiss. My curiosity mixed with the wine and the growing tingling sensation between my thighs encouraged me to give in to the man I had always wondered "what if" about. His lips finally touched mine and it turned out to be everything I fantasized it would be. His lips were succulent and juicy and they captivated my body. The next thing I knew his body was on top of mine with his hand creeping up my shirt. I realized that I still had on my sweaty workout clothes that I wore from earlier so I slightly pushed him off me. I think he misunderstood that as rejection but that clearly wasn't the case.

"What's wrong?" asked Demetri.

"Nothing at all I just want to take a shower first. I was just leaving the gym when I met up with you", I said as I took my socks off.

"Do you mind if I join you? On second thought, never mind. It may be too soon."

He hesitated a bit realizing that he had just ended his relationship earlier today so he didn't want to overstep his boundaries but this scenario is different for us. The feelings we had for each other from back then to now were mutual, and my raging hormones wouldn't have it any other way.

"Actually, you're welcome to join me if you'd like. That decision is totally up to you."

With that being said, I slowly unzipped my track jacket and let it drop to the floor. I took off my tank top shortly after and was left with my pink

Nike sports bra and yoga pants. I walked to the bathroom and turned the water on to let it heat up. I closed the door behind me and finished undressing before stepping into the shower. I left the door unlocked and anxiously waited in hopes that Demetri would decide to join me. I had already shaved my legs and washed up a few times when I heard my door slowly creak open. I had shampoo in my hair when he pulled my shower curtain back to expose his naked body. There he was standing as naked as the day he was born while I admired his body. He smirked when he seen my line of vision go from his pretty hazel eyes down to his dick. He wasn't fully standing at attention just yet but he wasn't small by any means. However, I knew that already. I had felt his dick before when we were dancing so I knew he wasn't lacking in the package department whatsoever but to see it in person was something different. Being a gym rat had done his body well. He was slim but muscular with a six pack, ample pecs and a deep V leading to his manhood. I was impressed and he knew it.

He confidently stepped into the shower behind me and wrapped his arms around my waist just like he did earlier, only this time we were naked and I could feel his dick throbbing on my lower back. He kissed the side of my neck and the water cascaded down his face. His hands cupped my breast then glided from my nipples and made their way between my thighs to massage my clit. The surges he sent through my body electrified me and charged my hormones. He eased his middle finger inside of me and hooked it into a position that hit a spot I forgot I had. I couldn't stop the moans from escaping my lips. My body wouldn't let me.

"I'm assuming from the moans I'm hearing that I found that spot", he whispers in my ear as he continued to kiss my neck. "I hope you're ready for what I have in store for you." I was on the brink of having an earth shattering orgasm when he abruptly stopped. He was driving me crazy and he knew it. He left me yearning for more. He rinsed the soap of his body and stepped out the shower. He wrapped a towel around his waist and smiled at me. "You know where to find me when you ready" he smirked and closed the door behind him. I couldn't wash that shampoo out of my hair fast enough. I hoped and prayed that I rinsed it all out. I stepped out of the shower and wrapped one towel around my hair and used another towel to dry off my body. With my hair still wrapped in the towel drying, I decided to lotion up with one of my favorite scents from Bath and Body Works. Once I finished moisturizing my body, I unraveled my towel and let my hair caress my back. It was still damp of course but that was fine with me. I wrapped a towel around my body and left the bathroom. I instantly heard slow music playing when I walked through the hallway leading to my bedroom. The lights were off and a few of my candles were lit. The shadow of the flames decorated the walls of my room as they flickered and danced. The thunderstorm outside was still going strong as the boom of the thunder scared the hell out of me. Surprisingly, my room was empty.

Suddenly, I felt arms wrapping around my waist and hands untying my towel from my body. I turned around to face the man that I've always wanted to be with secretly but my commitment to Tristan and the timing always seemed to be off until this moment. Usually having sex with anyone outside of marriage would be out of my character but I've always had a soft spot for Demetri so I couldn't help myself. My towel was around my ankles when I kissed his neck and stroked his dick with my hand. He quietly moaned at the tender touch of my hands. The liquor and wine removed my inhibitions as I found myself on my knees draping my lips around his dick. I had only gave head to my husband and it had been years since I did it so a part of me wanted to see if I still had it skills wise. It was like riding a bike, once you learn you never forget. Demetri ran his fingers through my hair and cupped the back of my head. I kept my rhythm as I engulfed more of him inch by inch. I felt his body become tense and his breath more rigid after a few minutes. I also found myself enjoying it more than I'd like. Knowing exactly what his gestures meant actually turned me on and made me not want to stop pleasing him. Before he could erupt he pulled himself away and grabbed my hand while leading me to the bed.

"It's not about me, tonight is all about you", he claimed as he climbed on top of me and nestled himself between my legs.

He kissed me from my lips and made a trail of kisses from my neck all the way down to my mound before stopping in between to show my nipples some attention. I felt his warm breath on my mound as he swirled his tongue around my clit and inserted his finger inside of me again. My breathing pattern instantly changed and became heavier as my hands embraced the back of his head and neck. He pushed my legs back and drove his tongue between my labia majora (or walls for those who don't know). I was in euphoria with the same intense sensation building up again. My thighs started to tremble and my moans grew louder. Here I lay on the edge of an orgasm again but suddenly he stops. He's clearly playing games with me now and knows that he has full control over my body. He lifts his head from between my legs and grins at me. He climbs on top of me and kiss my lips. I can smell my scent still lingering on his lips. I reach down in between my legs to grab his dick and slowly stroke him. He wasn't the only one that could take control so I propped myself on my knees to feel him throb in my mouth again. I circled the tip with my tongue and worked my way down his shaft. I relaxed my throat muscles and bobbed my head as if this was the best thing since sliced bread. I used my free hand to massage his balls. It wasn't long before he began to moan. His body tensed up as I heard his toes pop from curling. He enjoyed me giving him head for a few more minutes. He then gently pushed me away to lay me back on the bed.

"I told you tonight is all about you", he said as I laid there waiting on my back with my legs open for his invitation. He climbed on top of me and moaned in my ear as he slid the tip of his dick inside of me.

It had been so long that it was uncomfortable at first so he took his time to let my body adjust to his girth. Outside of having a little fun with my vibrator every blue moon, I was celibate. His thrusts was slow and deliberate as I arched my back and tilted my head releasing passionate and lustful moans. My legs were wrapped around his waist as he maneuvered his way in and out of me. We both moaned in unison and it felt as if my soul was intertwining with his. He shifted his weight and rested on his elbows as he vengefully connected his lips with mine. I couldn't help but bite down on his lower lip as I felt that familiar wave of pleasure begin to boil inside of me once again making my legs tremble. Demetri noticed my face twisting in ecstasy and my orgasm approaching so he bit down on my right shoulder. How did he know that a little pain with pleasure was my weakness and a major turn on? That pushed me over the edge as my eyes rolled to the back of my head and I sunk my nails deep into his lower back while by body quivered from the effects of his thrusts. I felt my wetness between my thighs and on his pelvis as he continued to please me. My body was still trembling when Demetri pulled out and flipped me over to my knees to enter me from behind. I don't know what came over him, but the slow deliberate strokes were replaced with fast paced strokes that I never really experienced with my late husband.

The way Demetri was handling my body turned me on to no end. He gripped my hips and continued hitting it from the back. He ran his hand through my hair and pulled a handful of it causing my head to jerk back in pure pleasure as we both moaned. I didn't expect him to have such a sexy moan. I was nearing my second orgasm when I felt his body stiffen up and his breath become shaky. I looked back at him to find his eyes closed and him biting down on his lower lip. He looked so sexy with his face scrunched up in ecstasy. He let go of my hair and caressed my neck. His touch soon became a grip which grew tighter as his moans became louder with every stroke pushing him closer to his climax. With one hand still wrapped around my neck and the other gripping my hip, he bit down on my shoulder again and it sent me over the edge once more. I whimpered in delight as he pulled out of me and came on my lower back before collapsing on top of me exhausted from pleasure. We stayed in that position for a few moments to catch our breaths while he ever so lightly kissed the nape of my neck and my right shoulder multiple times in between his gasps for air. I couldn't help but think about all of the sexual dreams that I had about him before realizing that this was so much better. After regaining his breath, he finally rolled over to lie on his back. He got up and went to the bathroom to grab a towel and clean up the mess we had just made. I was still laying on my stomach when he returned to wipe off my lower back. I felt totally comfortable being completely naked in front of him. No words were spoken for a while. We just enjoyed each other's presence. We were still absolutely naked when he pulled my silk sheets over his torso and nudged me closer to him to cuddle up against his strong chest. I felt totally relaxed as if this wasn't our first intimate moment together. I abruptly felt the urge to pee so I sat up and pulled the covers back.

"Hey, where are you going?" he finally spoke.

"I'm just going to the bathroom. I'll be back." I smiled at his possessiveness over me.

"After what we just did I wasn't worried about that", he grinned.

"Boy hush, I'll be back in a second", I said as I crawled out of bed still completely naked and of course he watched me as I sashayed out of the room.

I strolled down the hallway to my bathroom and flicked on the light. I took a glimpse in the mirror and seen that my hair was a hot mess. I grabbed my brush and a rubber band so I could put my hair in a high bun before washing my face and freshening up a bit. When I returned to the bedroom I noticed that Demetri was asleep and snoring lightly. I couldn't help but have a flashback of my late husband sleeping in that same spot and snoring. For some reason I felt a bit of guilt creeping up as if I had committed infidelity and before I knew it the water works were running down my cheeks as I ran back to the bathroom to wipe my tears. It took a moment but I pulled myself together and returned back to my room. Demetri was still slightly snoring. I pushed the sheets back and seen that he was still naked as the day he was born. I smiled and slid in next to him. Without any hesitation, he pulled me closer to his chest, wrapped his arm around my waist, and placed his foot in between mine. I forgot what it felt like to cuddle after good sex. I leaned in towards him and kissed him on the lips before drifting off to sleep.

Chapter Four:

Kelsey

I woke up around 6:30 A.M the next day. Being an early bird always allowed me to naturally wake up early even on my off days. I crooked my neck back at Demetri who was still sleeping and snoring. I decided to take a quick shower while he was still knocked out. I opted to wear something comfortable when I got dressed so I put on some yoga pants and a matching top. I brushed my hair into another bun before going to the kitchen. I figured Demetri may need some breakfast to help subside the hangover I'm sure he'll be nurturing whenever he wakes up. I was just putting the finishing touches on my special vegetable and cheese omelet when he entered the kitchen. He looked refreshed as if he had just showered and he was wearing the clothes I left folded for him in the bathroom.

"That food smells so good that it actually woke me up out of my sleep which isn't an easy task to do. What's for breakfast?" he asked as he took a seat on the barstool next to the island in my kitchen.

"Well, I had a taste for a cheese omelet so I made a vegetable and cheese omelet with turkey bacon and a berry smoothie. You got a hangover?" I asked facetiously, already knowing the answer.

"Yeah, my head's pounding. That's my body's way of telling me that I'm not a drinker. What about you?"

"I'm good actually. I only had a few mixed drinks. You, on the other hand, were drinking straight shots with no chaser", I smirked at him.

"Yeah, and I'm regretting that now", he claimed while returning my smirk.

"Did you regret last night?" I inquired trying to see where his mind was after our "night cap."

"No. Why would I regret last night when I'd been waiting years for this to happen. I really enjoyed last night. I hope I didn't hurt you though. It's been a while and I was a little excited." I tried to make eye contact with him but he looked away as if he was embarrassed.

He had a look of concern sketched across his face. He was referring to the biting, choking and hair pulling from last night's events correctly assuming that I wasn't used to that type of treatment. My husband was a missionary position type of man who preferred to take his time instead of rushing. However, I was infatuated with how Demetri manhandled my body roughly and delicately all at the same time. Yeah, he handled my body damn well last night so he shouldn't have a damn thing to be embarrassed about.

"Actually, you were a little rough but I enjoyed every minute of it. Even though I've never been handled like that before, it turned me on how you took care of my body so you have nothing to be ashamed about", I reassured him.

"Well, that's good to know. I woke up thinking I probably scared the hell out of you!" he laughed.

"It takes more than that to scare me Demetri", I said sharing a laugh with him.

I finished making his plate and sat it down in front of him. His eyes lit up like a kid in the candy store. I sat down in front of him and started eating my food. I've never seen a man eat so fast in my life. I had to ask was he in a rush to go somewhere.

"You're eating like you haven't eaten in days. You got somewhere that you need to be soon?"

"No, it's just been a long time since I had a home cooked breakfast."

"Wow, it's been a long time since you had breakfast at home? How long has it been since you've had sex?" I was curious of course.

"You really want to know?"

"Well, yes. We have been intimate."

"In the last six months I've only had sex four times. Does that answer your question?" he continued eating.

"Yeah, it does. No wonder you couldn't control yourself", I had to giggle.

"While you're over there laughing at me when was the last time you had sex?"

"The night Tristan died. December 27th, 2009. Seven years to be exact, up until last night." I looked down at my ring finger again out of habit.

"I'm sorry. Forget that I even asked."

"No, it's okay. I'm fine now. I can finally talk about his death without driving myself crazy."

"Still, on a lighter note, what are your plans for tonight?"

"I'm going to my son's basketball game. You're welcome to come of course."

"Yeah, I'll be there. I just have to check on my mom first. She just got released from the hospital yesterday. Do you want to ride together to the game?" His brown eyes made contact with mine and I melted inside.

"I hope your mom is doing well, but yeah you can pick me up from here. The game starts at seven tonight so I'll be ready by 6:30."

"Alright, I'll be here. Are you going to introduce me to Tristan?"

"Normally I wouldn't but we got history and since I know you and your family I don't have a problem with that."

"I hope he likes me", he said as he continued eating.

"I think he will. Only time will tell though." I was trying to be optimistic but I know TJ is very protective of me so their introduction could be either peaches and cream or could go from sugar to shit real quick knowing TJ's temper.

We finished our breakfast and lounged around the house for a bit before he left to check on his mother. I found myself shocked when I started missing him shortly thereafter. However, I used this alone time to clean my house, pick out an outfit for the game, check on my son and catch up with Kendra. I decided to call TJ first. He answered on the second ring.

"Hey Ma, what you been up to? You didn't even answer your phone when I called you last night."

"Well, hello to you too. If you must know I recently reconnected with an old friend and we went out last night." I found myself smiling just at the mere thought of Demetri.

"Is this friend of yours a dude?"

"Yes, he is and he's joining me at your game tonight." I said proudly.

"Really Ma? I don't need to be worried about you and some random dude all lovey-dovey in the stands while I'm trying to focus on the game", he said with too much attitude and tone of voice for my liking.

"First of all, watch your tone when you're talking to me. Secondly, I wouldn't introduce you to a random guy. He's an old friend from college. Your father and Kendra know him."

"How did my pops know this clown again?"

"Didn't I tell you to watch your tone TJ? I'm not playing with you. We all went to college together", I said defensively.

"Are you interested in this friend being more than just a friend?"

"Actually, I am very interested in him being more than just a friend so when I introduce him to you I expect you to have the respect I raised you to have. Do you understand me?"

"Yeah Ma I understand. I got some homework to finish so I'll see you at the game. Love you."

"I love you too.

I never knew how TJ would react whenever I decided to date again which is why I never dated anyone after Tristan passed away. I didn't want to bring anyone around my son until he was a lot older. Besides, there weren't many men I was even remotely interested in until I reconnected with Demetri. I should have expected him to be overprotective because it's just been us ever since his father passed but now there's another man in the picture and he has to cope with it not being his father. After I finished cleaning my house I finally got around to calling Kendra.

“Hey, what’s up girl?” asked Kendra.

“I just had the best night of my life.”

“What happened?”

“So, Demetri called me last night and asked me to meet him at this bar. I agreed because he sounded stressed out and I’m not gonna lie, I missed him too. Well, long story short, he came back to my house for a night cap and before you fix your mouth to ask, yes he is single now and... I just had the best sex ever!” I was smiling from ear to ear.

“Wow, somebody finally had the honors of clearing out those cobwebs? Girl I’m so proud of you! I want details! Was the ‘D’ little?” She seemed even more excited than I was at the moment.

“Come on Kendra, why do you need to know the details? Wouldn’t that be too much information?”

“Hell no! It’s not every day that I hear you tell me that you just had the best sex of your life. Plus you always ask me for details about my friends and I never hesitate to inform you. Now spill it!”

"Alright, since you insist. No, he wasn't little by any means. Surprisingly, he was rougher than I imagined him to be", I finally admitted.

"You saying that like you never had rough sex before?"

"Up until last night, I hadn't."

"If you were to ask me that is the best type of sex to have. Hell, that's all I know to be honest. I don't have time for the slow lovey-dovey bullshit."

"See, that's where I disagree. Don't knock it until you try it Kendra."

"I've never been in love to make love with someone so I get mines and I keep it moving."

"One day you're going to meet someone who's going to change you. How was that ride for you and Marcus?" It was my turn to be nosy.

"There was no riding other than the ride we took from the restaurant to my place. I'm not gonna lie, when he dropped me off the other night, I was going to put it on him but then I thought about that conversation we had and changed my mind. I decided to make him earn it. You should be proud of me." She beamed as if she deserved a gold star for good behavior or something.

"Of course I am. I'm surprised you actually listened. I thought my words were falling on deaf ears."

"I heard you. I just hate it when you try to preach to me. Everyone can't be a prude like you Kelsey", she giggled.

"Whatever, I only preach to you like that because I care about your well-being."

"Yeah, I know and I appreciate that. So, what are you doing later?"

"I'm going to TJ's game. You were supposed to be coming with me too remember?"

"Damn, I forgot and already made plans to go out and eat with Marcus tonight."

"It's cool. Demetri is coming with me anyway."

"So you plan on introducing him to Tristan?"

"Yeah, I am. Do you think it's too soon?"

"I mean, it's not like Demetri is a stranger and Tristan is a kid. I say go for it."

"I told him about Demetri earlier when we talked and he was clearly upset about it."

"He'll get over it Kelsey. You've sacrificed enough and it's time for you to be happy again."

"Yeah, you got a point."

"Girl, I have to start getting ready for this date so I'll call you later."

"Alright, don't forget what I'm telling you either. Bye."

It was still early in the day so I decided to run to the gym and get a quick workout in. I was a little sore from last night, but I pushed through my work out. I couldn't help but smile to myself as I thought about Demetri.

Chapter Five:

Demetri

I pulled up to my parents' house shortly after I left Kelsey's place. I took a cab home to get one of my cars since the other one was still at the bar. I felt like a new man as I rang the doorbell and waited for someone to answer. I could have let myself in with my house key but the last time I did that, I caught my parents in the middle of having sex. I know that's how I got here but I damn sure didn't want to witness that up close and personal again. I definitely learned that lesson quick. My mom opened the door and kissed me on the cheek. She was smiling from ear to ear.

"Why are you cheesing so hard, Ma? Your face is going to get stuck like that if you keep it up", I joked with her.

"I'm smiling because you came here glowing like a pregnant woman. I'm guessing you and Kelsey got reacquainted like I suggested?"

"What makes you think that?" I tried to wipe the "I got some cutty last night" grin off my face so she wouldn't notice.

"Well for one, you smell like you showered with a woman's scent and two, those aren't your clothes. Jogging pants and sweatshirts isn't your style", my mom proclaimed as she took a seat on the sofa.

"I hate it when you read me like a book." I had to chuckle because I could never put anything past my mother.

"You're my flesh and blood so of course I should be able to read you. Did you close one door before you opened the other?" She always spoke in cryptic messages but as my mom, I always understood her.

"Of course Ma, you didn't raise me to be a cheater."

"So, let me get this straight. You broke up with Karma yesterday, and slept with Kelsey the same night?"

"What makes you think I slept with Kelsey?"

"Am I wrong Demetri?"

"No, Ma." Ever since I was a kid she stressed honesty no matter what so we always had an open line of communication. If my mama wanted to know anything from me, all she had to do was ask. I can admit that I'm a bit of a mama's boy, so what?

"Did you use protection?" she inquired.

"Come on, now you getting too personal, Ma. Where's Pops?" I had to change the subject because I didn't want to have to explain to her how I failed to use a condom.

"He went to grab us something to eat. I wasn't up to cooking and you know your father can burn water. He'll be back soon."

I heard my dad coming through the back door with bags of food and a tray of drinks. He looked as if he was struggling so I grabbed the bags of food to give him a hand. Looking at my dad was like looking in the mirror because I was a spitting image of him; all the way from the hazel eyes to the height and body structure. The only difference is our childhood experiences. Unlike my experience growing up privileged, my father grew up in the hood of Milwaukee, Wisconsin with a single mother and a criminal past. He always appreciated the fact that my mother had changed him for the better in multiple ways. The old man still looked good though. You'd never catch him dressed down. I don't think he even owned a pair of jogging pants.

"I can carry bags of food. I'm not handicapped you know, and what the hell are you wearing?" My dad was the complete opposite of my mother. He wasn't a big fan of showing emotions.

"I didn't stay home last night so this was all I had to wear."

"Where were you last night?" My Pops cross-examined me like a witness on the stand.

"I was at Kelsey's house last night."

"Yeah, your mother told me that you two had been hanging out but damn you move fast!" My Pops laughed.

"It didn't make sense for me to wait. This is the first time she's been single since I've known her. Plus, I've had enough of Karma's mind games and lies."

"Well, good riddance to her. I never liked her anyway", pops proclaimed.

"It's funny how no one liked her but failed to tell me."

"That's not true. You know I told you every chance I got", my mom chimed in.

"You're a grown ass man, Demetri. There's no need for me to hold your hand like you're still a kid."

"Yeah, you're right. I was just stopping by to check on you guys. I got a date so I'll stop by some other time." I hugged my mama before I left and closed the door behind me.

I left my parent's house and headed to my condo. When I pulled into my driveway, I got an eerie feeling. Shit! I forgot the locksmith was coming this morning to change my locks. My front door was cracked open when I pulled my house keys out. I instantly knew that Karma's ass must have been bailed out of jail. I opened the door and realized that my place was completely trashed. My sheets were ripped apart, glass was everywhere, and all of my clothes had been bleached. So much for me changing clothes. I went to the bathroom and seen that she had written "asshole" on my mirror in red lipstick. I felt a headache creeping up on me. I glanced at the clock and seen that it was almost five in the evening. I pulled my phone out and rescheduled my appointment for the locksmith to come back out tomorrow. I left and locked up my apartment so I could go grab some clothes from the mall. I was pissed about my tailored suits being bleached. That shit isn't cheap! I don't have time to be pissed though. I didn't want to be late picking up Kelsey for the game. I was already looking forward to seeing her again and it hadn't even been a full day of us being apart. I was acting "whipped" already.

I bought a few button-up shirts, jeans, slacks, beaters, and briefs to wear in the meantime until I could get some more tailored suits. I also purchased some more cologne too. Karma had bought the scent I was currently wearing as a gift and I didn't want any more ties to her. I made a mental note to throw that shit out whenever I made it back to my place. I stopped at my barbershop to get another crispy lining and tapered haircut before heading over to Kelsey's house. Her truck must have still been at the bar because I didn't see it when I pulled up. I was whipping my second favorite car which was the latest model of the Buick Lacrosse. I could definitely afford a more luxurious car but there was something about this car that was so sexy to me.

I walked to the porch and rang the doorbell. She opened the door after a few moments. She looked beautiful as always. She was wearing a peach cardigan with a tan scarf, jeans, and tan boots. She had on gold hoop earrings and her hair was in another bun. I assumed that was her favorite hairstyle. I noticed that she didn't have on any make up. Her face was flawless. She never really needed anything more than mascara and lipstick… if that. Marcus would most likely call me soft for noticing the small details of her beauty, but my mother raised me to pay attention to a woman and appreciate a real woman's exquisiteness inside and out. The look in her eyes told me that I wasn't looking too bad myself.

"You ready to go?" I asked her.

"Yeah, I'm ready. You look nice by the way", she said smiling at me.

Wow, a woman that actually give compliments instead of always expecting them. Believe it or not, men like some reassurance every now and then too. Most women often forget that. I think I'm in love.

"You look beautiful too. Nice outfit."

"Thanks. So did you catch a cab here?"

"No, I went home and grabbed my other car. It's out front."

Even though it was a short distance we walked to the car hand in hand. I unlocked the doors and opened the passenger side for her and of course she thanked me. As I sat behind the wheel, she told me that there was something sexy about my car. I smirked to myself because great minds think alike.

"I must admit that I'm a little nervous about you and Tristan meeting. When I told him that you were coming to the game with me he got upset."

"Well, that's to be expected. He probably thinks that I'm trying to replace his father. It's cool though, I can definitely handle pressure so don't stress over it." I placed my hand on her thigh to reassure her.

"Yeah, you're right. I'll just let the situation play out."

We enjoyed some old school R&B music while we drove to Tristan's high school. Being next to her was like a breath of fresh air. Hell being around a woman who doesn't always cop an attitude for no reason was a breath of fresh air. I thought to myself as I snuck a few glances at her on the sly while I was driving. Now I see what my Pops was talking about when he first met my mother. If I could get what my parents have I'll die a satisfied man. If a person ever tells you that they don't need love and want to be team single for the rest of their days, don't believe it. Everybody needs somebody; even a womanizer like Marcus.

The parking lot was packed to capacity when we arrived. I pulled out my wallet out and paid the admissions fees when we reached the entry gate. I must have forgotten what high school was like because these kids were definitely of a different breed. These high school girls looked like grown ass women. From what Kelsey told me TJ was still a virgin and looking at how these girls were dressed now he should keep it that way. It was live when we entered the gym; Jay-Z and Kanye West "Ball So Hard" record was blasting throughout the gym while the two teams warmed up. I noticed Tristan immediately out of all the players. Despite the fact that he was the tallest player on his team, he resembled his father a lot more than he did Kelsey. He smiled when he seen Kelsey but this smile quickly faded when we made eye contact. I can understand why though. I'm over protective over my mother too.

Kelsey and I took a seat in the stands where we could see all the action. The game started with TJ's team winning the jump ball toss, and immediately TJ started off with an explosive dunk that excited the crowd and brought them to their feet. I was impressed to say the least, but I couldn't help but feel as if that explosiveness was to send me a message because as soon as he landed on his feet, he stared me right in the eyes with a mug sketched across his face. Little did he know that it would take more than a mean mug to scare me away from his mother.

The rest of the game was quite entertaining. Tristan's team won in double overtime by three points and TJ walked away with a triple-double game. He definitely had skills and talent which reminded me of his father in college when he played basketball. Kelsey and I waited for him by the exit door while he talked to a few scouts.

"I have to run to the ladies room. I'll be back", Kelsey informed me.

TJ had just finished talking to a scout when he decided to make his way over to me. I could tell by the mug on his face that this wasn't going to be a friendly conversation. When he did finally approach me, we stood eye to eye.

"Man to man, what are your intentions with my mother?" I guess introductions were out of the question, I thought to myself.

"My intentions are to make her my wife and the mother of my kids one day", I claimed with certainty.

"I'm sure you got some hood-rat baby mamas walking around here somewhere so how about you talk to one of them instead?"

"I don't do the whole baby mama thing. That's not my style and I don't have any kids by the way. My name is Demetri Latimore too, just in case you were wondering."

"Yeah, and? I already know who you are. So from what I hear, you knew my father."

"Yeah, we went to college together."

"And you expect me to be cool with you pushing up on my mother when you knew my father?" His disdain for me was evident but that didn't scare me whatsoever.

"Since you wanted a man to man conversation, I'm going to give it to you. When I met your mother, she was already involved with your father. I had deep feelings for her despite the fact that she was already taken but I respected their relationship and even tried to move on up until recently. And now that I have the opportunity to genuinely love your mother as much as your father did are you going to get in the way of that or are you going to let her be happy like she deserves?" He paused as he thought about my question for a moment.

"Of course I want her to be happy. I respect your honesty but if you break her heart, I'll be breaking your jaw. Understood?" he threatened with his fists balled and his jawline clenched.

I was about to respond to what he said until Kelsey approached us smiling. She hugged him and congratulated him on the win.

“I might have a full scholarship with the Kentucky Wildcats if I keep playing like this for the rest of the season. Their head coach is really feeling me”, he announced with a smile on his face to Kelsey as if he hadn’t just threaten me.

“That’s good but Kentucky is kind of far from Wisconsin. What about Marquette University? A lot of great athletes attended there and moved on to have great careers.”

“Yeah, you have a point, but I don’t know if I want to stay in Wisconsin Ma.”

“We’ll talk about it later. You still have the rest of the season to worry about anyway. By the way, Demetri this is my son Tristan. Tristan, this is the Demetri, my friend I told you about earlier.”

“I know Ma. We got real acquainted already.” He made eye contact with me again to get his point across, or at least that’s what I’m guessing.

“Should I be worried about that?” asked Kelsey.

“Not at all. He and I have an understanding”, I reassured her.

"So, what's the plan for you tonight TJ?" Kelsey asked.

"Well, coach is taking the team out to eat since we had a good game. Then I'm sleeping over Troy's house tonight because we have an early practice and he needs a ride."

"Can you let me know when you make it there safely?"

"Yeah, I always do. It was nice meeting you, Mr. Latimore. Remember what I said too." Tristan kissed Kelsey on the cheek and then went inside the boy's locker room.

"What exactly did he say to you?" inquired Kelsey.

"It's nothing really major. We just had a little heart to heart. He's really mature for his age. I thought I was talking to a grown ass man for a second", I chuckled to lighten the mood.

"I don't know if that's a good thing or a bad thing. He never really got the chance to enjoy being a kid. He matured too fast in my opinion."

"You sure he's still a virgin?" I asked to make sure because he seemed too mature to be a virgin in my opinion.

"Yeah, I'm positive. We talk about everything. Tristan told me that he and his father had a conversation that he'd never forget before he passed away."

"What was that if you don't mind me asking?" I opened the passenger door for her again when we made it back to my car.

"He told him: 'the presence of women is going to always be there waiting but the opportunity to excel athletically and academically isn't. Stay focused on those two things and I promise you'll get far. A quality woman will come into the picture when the time is right, and if you need to know what a quality woman looks like just look at your mother.' Those were his exact words."

I saw tears welling in the corner of her eye while she looked out the window. Maybe I shouldn't have asked that question but my curiosity got the best of me. I'll make a mental note of avoiding the topic of Tristan senior in the future. If I wasn't driving I would absolutely be consoling her.

"Are you okay?"

"Not really. I love seeing TJ play ball but every time I do, I have a flashback of me watching Tristan play at our high school and college games. They look so much alike that it's scary sometimes."

"Yeah, he looks nothing like you but you have to remember that he's not Tristan."

"I know. I've gotten a lot better over the years. You should have seen me before. I remember the days when I avoided seeing my own child because looking at him was like watching the ghost of his father. I was battling depression then but I'm mentally healthy now, thanks to the Most High."

"Well, I'm glad to hear that. If you need a shoulder to cry on or an open ear, you know I'm here right?"

"Yeah, I know and I appreciate that. Since I have an empty nest tonight, would you like to spend the night again?"

"Of course. My girlfriend shouldn't even have to ask me to spend the night. You would think that would be a known fact", I flirted.

"Did you just call me your girlfriend?" she smiled.

"Yeah, I thought that was a known fact too?"

"And when did you decide to think that?" she flirted back.

"I decided that last night when I entered you raw and uncut. But if you want to get technical, you were my girl long before you even realized it."

"So you was peeping me hard on some stalker shit, uh?" she laughed.

"I mean, yeah if that's what you want to call it. Okay I may have been a borderline stalker in college. I'm not too proud to admit it but let us not forget that you were feeling me too." I was laying my game on thick. Maybe it was because I was looking good and feeling better. A good woman with better pussy would do that to man's ego.

We finally made it back to her place. She claimed she was definitely going to the bar to get her car for sure tomorrow, but I think she enjoyed me chauffeuring her around the city too much to do that. Once we were inside her place, we chilled and watched a movie on her sofa but the movie was mainly watching us. She was talking as if she didn't know that she was now my girlfriend, but she finally admitted that she was happy I had declared her officially off the dating market. I was already thinking of ways to propose to her. She deserved more than the girlfriend title. I've always wanted her to have my last name so I was going to make that happen soon. She decided to take her hair out of the bun that I had grown accustomed to liking. As she removed her bun, her curls fell loose onto her face and shoulders. She looked so angelic. She smiled when she caught me staring at her.

"What are you thinking about?" she asked as she tilted her head.

I didn't even answer the question. I leaned in and kissed her. I don't think she realized how soft her lips really were. I wanted her bad as ever and I wanted to step up and be the man that she has always deserved. No words were spoken after that question; at least not any audible words. Instead, I let my body do all of the talking for me. She climbed on top of me and cupped my face in her hands. I sat back on the sofa and decided to let her take control this time. She kissed a tender spot on my neck and ran her hands up my chest. Her tongue and hands felt as if they were created just for me. She slowly unbuttoned my shirt then stripped me out of my pants. I was left in my briefs with her on top of me in a matching bra and panties set. I know this may be petty but it really irritates me when a woman's bra and panties don't match. I'd prefer them to match because it shows me that you care about how you present yourself to a man. Plus, it's just a complete turn on for me.

She kneeled down in between my legs and pulled my briefs off. I can tell she enjoyed giving oral sex as much as I did because I didn't even have to ask her to do it. She gladly volunteered and I didn't resist. She did things with her tongue that I can't even verbally explain and my toes started cramping from constantly curling. I was a little embarrassed when I found myself moaning like a chick but I couldn't help it though. Like the rap artist J. Cole said, "I love it when you give me head; I hate it when you give me headaches." Kelsey didn't strike me as the type of woman to give a man a headache though. She was more like the medicine to relieve it. She stood up and slowly undressed for me. She unhooked her bra and let it fall to the floor. She made eye contact with me the entire time as she pulled her panties down and tossed them on my chest. My head was still spinning from her head game. I always suspected that she was an undercover freak but now I knew for sure. I relished in the idea that only one other man knew what this type of heaven was like while it was a mystery to the brothers who wanted to see for themselves. Too bad they'll never know.

She climbed back on top of me and eased down on my dick slowly. I bit down on my lower lip to keep from moaning like a female. She caught a rhythm that told me she was in it for the long haul. I've never been a minute man but she made it hard for me to control myself. I definitely wasn't going to be able to control myself with her riding me like this and her breast swaying in front of me. I picked her up from the couch and continued the rhythm she created for us. I didn't miss a beat either. She had her arms wrapped around my neck when she started kissing me while still riding my dick even though we were standing up. I was losing control again especially when I felt her muscles contracting on my shit. If she didn't have her tongue in my mouth right now I would definitely be moaning like a chick.

I bent my knees, lowered myself to the floor and gently laid her down on her back on top of her plush carpet, not once pulling out. Why should I pull out when I never wanted to leave my new home, are you crazy? Now I was back in control and wanted to handle her body the best way I knew how. I wasn't used to the missionary position. I'm honestly more of an ass man so I would prefer back shots but seeing her many different faces made it so worth it. I stroked her as deep as my anatomy would allow while enjoying the moans I heard escaping from her lips. I knew she was about to come when I felt her nails scratching my lower back and her loves muscles contracting on my dick again. Her face was scrunched in pleasure when she came and moaned my name in my ear. I don't think she knew how many times I'd fantasized about this particular moment. The wetness from her love and that last contraction had my head spinning to the point where I couldn't control myself any longer. I gave her one long stroke and pulled out before busting on her plush white carpet. She made eye contact with me and smirked.

“What’s so funny?” I asked her. I had after shock like something serious. I had to catch my breath.

“Nothing, I just hope you plan on cleaning that up”, she laughed.

“I always clean up my mess baby”, I said to her as I stood up. I can tell she had some type of OCD. Everything in her house had to be organized and clean.

When I got the energy, I went to the bathroom and grabbed a small towel. I wet it with some warm water and soap to clean up my mess as she put it earlier. When I got back to the living room she was still laying in the same spot that I had left her in. The way she smiled at me and my nakedness made me want to go for round two but my body was already drained from round one. I couldn’t help but think that neither one of us had thought to use protection again. Last night I could have blamed it on the alcohol but I didn’t have any excuses for tonight. My mother would be looking at me like I had two heads if I were ever to tell her that. We took a shower together after that and really watched the movie from earlier this time. She laid her head on my chest and seemed really interested in the movie. I, on the other hand, was more interested in looking at her. I ran my fingers through her hair and thought to myself that this was it for me. How could any man in his right mind not want this?

We ended up falling asleep on the couch and the next morning I woke up to an empty couch and the smell of breakfast. I could get used to eating home cooked meals on a daily basis. I went to the bathroom to wash my face and brush my teeth. I was only wearing briefs and a beater but I had my clothes in the trunk of my car to change this time. I walked inside the kitchen where she was making French toast and singing a song that I'd never heard before. Seeing her happy, genuinely made me happier. I walked up behind her and wrapped my arms around her waist and kissed her on the cheek.

"How did you sleep?" she asked.

"I slept so good that I don't even remember when I fell asleep."

"You want some breakfast?"

"Come on, that's like asking a fish do they need water", I joked with her.

"Yeah, dumb question huh? You got any plans today?"

"Yeah, I have to go back to my place to meet the locksmith soon. I would invite you to visit but it's trashed thanks to Karma."

"How do you know it was her?" she asked as she flipped the toast.

"Because she still has keys and I haven't had the chance to change the locks. It wasn't like my place was broken into. The door frame was still intact. Plus, there aren't too many burglars that write "asshole" on mirrors in lipstick."

"I thought you had a restraining order on her?"

"I do, and if she violates the order I'll make sure I handle it so don't worry about it", I assured her.

"Okay, I trust that you'll handle it. Can you drop me off to my car before you go home?"

"Yeah, just let me finish this breakfast first."

I got dressed after we ate, dropped Kelsey off to her car and gave her a kiss before I pulled off. I was running late on meeting the locksmith and I hated being late to anything. When I pulled up a young black dude was waiting by my front door. He didn't look like a locksmith to me.

"Can I help you?"

"You want your locks changed right? I've been waiting here for twenty minutes. You lucky I decided to wait", he said with an attitude. I ignored what looked like a teenager to me and unlocked my door. The young man couldn't get over how fucked up my apartment was.

"You must have really pissed off some chick for her to fuck up your place like this. Nigga, changing locks not gonna stop this chick. My man you need to change addresses, not locks", he stated as he continued to look around.

"Dude, just shut up and do what I paid for you to come here and do so you can leave."

"No offense, I was just trying to give you some advice. I've been here before too. If you got that good 'D' this is to be expected. I'm just saying man to man."

"How long is this process going to take?"

"I'll be out of your hair in about ten minutes."

"Good." I was getting really irritated with him.

"In the meantime you should take my advice."

"No, I'm good. I can handle this."

"Alright, I see you like learning the hard way. Here's the paperwork I need you to sign, and here are your new keys. Take care." The young guy left just as quickly as he came.

As he left, I started cleaning up my apartment. It took me about two hours to get everything back in order. I'll replace my vases and televisions later. I locked my house back up and headed to the car so I could make my way back to Kelsey's.

"Where do you think you're going Demetri? You going back to your new bitch house? That's going to be kind of hard to do with flat tires, isn't it?" Karma announced as she sat on the hood of my car with a knife in her hands.

"I put a restraining order on your crazy ass for a reason. Now leave me the fuck alone Karma."

This bitch keyed my car and slashed my tires. I've never used the term bitch to describe a female but that seemed to be the only word that suited her. I needed to get to my other car but I didn't want Kelsey anywhere near this situation so I called Marcus instead to come pick me up. Then I went back inside my apartment so I could calm down and avoid killing Karma's crazy ass. I also called my Pops once I made it inside.

“Hello.”

“Pops, are you busy?”

“No, I’m just going over some paperwork. What’s up?”

“You still got friends in high places?”

“Yeah, of course I do. What happened now?”

“Karma is here outside my apartment. She slashed my tires and keyed my car. I already had Judge Wilkerson put a restraining order on her but I feel like I’m losing control of the situation and I might do something to her that I’ll regret”, I told my pops through clenched teeth.

“Don’t worry about it. I’ll handle it. Just make sure you stay away from that girl.”

“How do you plan on handling it?”

“Don’t worry about it Demetri. In the meantime, I suggest you start looking for another place to live.”

“It’s funny that you mentioned that because the locksmith just told me that before he left.”

“That must be a smart man?”

“I doubt it. He seemed more like a little boy. I could still smell the breast milk on his breath.”

"Well, he must have pissed off some chick too", Pops laughed

"Dad, I got to go. Marcus just pulled up. Thanks for handling this."

"No problem son. Be safe out there."

I locked up my apartment again before I left. Karma's crazy ass was still sitting on the hood of my car, waiting. Although she still looked good, I knew she was just a devil in a blue dress. She started up again with another one of her temper tantrums when I walked passed her without even acknowledging her presence.

"So, I see you changed the locks like that's gonna stop me from coming around. Don't act like you don't fucking hear me Demetri. I spent the whole fucking night in jail because of you! You forgot that I have friends in high places too? Wait until I find out who the bitch is that you been fucking with Demetri!" she screamed as she jumped off of the hood of my car to follow me.

I couldn't hop in Marcus's car fast enough. She was turning my day from sugar to shit with her bullshit. Marcus burned rubber when he pulled off since she was trying to open the passenger door.

"What the hell did you do to her for her to be tripping like that? She better be lucky she missed my car with that brick. I'm not you, I will hit her ass!" Marcus was pissed. I knew that his car was his baby.

"I changed the locks on her ass and moved on. She was already crazy when I met her. I had no hand in that."

"So, what are you going to do about the Buick?"

"I'm going to get it to the shop and have it repaired. I'm pressing charges again since she wants to keep vandalizing my shit and I may need a few favors from some of your friends at the department in the future."

"Just give me the word on when you need it and consider it handled. You know the captain is my frat brother."

"Alright, I'm going to hold you to that. How was your date with Kendra though?"

"It was pretty cool. We got a lot in common and she's cool to kick back with", he stated calmly.

"Did you hit it?" I expected him to say yes.

"Hell no! She wasn't having it and trust me when I say I was trying. I was laying my game on thick and flirting my ass off. I was saying all the right things. She still wasn't going for it."

"I think the player has finally lost his mojo", I laughed.

"Hell no! That won't be happening around these parts. It's just a matter of time that's all. While you worried about me, you need to be worried about miss holier-than-thou Kelsey. You have to damn near marry her before you can even smell the pussy", Marcus laughed.

"I smelled it already while you talking shit about my woman", I joked with him.

"What! Nigga don't tell me that you're pussy whipped already? It's only been what, two weeks since you reconnected her? You've always been soft when it comes to women."

"So, I'm soft because I treat women with respect and don't fuck everything that moves like you?" Now I was getting defensive.

"You know that's a lie. I don't fuck everything that moves. If she's ugly I'm not fucking with her. And you're soft because you fall in love every five minutes." Marcus laughed again not realizing that I was becoming irritated with him.

“I’ve only been in love with two women and Karma’s ass doesn’t count anymore.”

“So, you’re really in love with Kelsey?”

“Yeah, you got a problem with that?”

“No, if anything I’m actually happy for you. It’s only been about twenty years since you’ve been chasing her.” He got jokes today I see.

“Going Greek was what kept you from falling in love in college. Your head got bigger when you got your letters, you know that right?” I must have pushed a button because he suddenly stopped joking.

“Don’t come at my frat like that bro. I’m a Phi Beta Sigma man until I die. Bitches love the brothers in blue and that’s not my fault.” Marcus yelled their infamous roll call.

“We not in college anymore bro! You can chill with the roll call”, I laughed.

“Yeah, whatever. I told you that I’m blue until the day I die and I’m gone always represent.”

We finally made it to the bar where my car had been parked. Marcus told me that he and Kendra were going bowling tonight so he would catch up with me later. I drove back to Kelsey’s to spend the rest of the weekend with her before it was back to work on Monday. I never worked weekends. That was the beauty of having your own business. You make your own schedule and come and go as you please.

Chapter Six:

Marcus

I thought about some of the things that Demetri said to me on my way back to my bachelors pad. He had a point when it came to how I treated women and not having much respect for them. I've never met a woman that gave me a reason to respect her. I didn't grow up in a loving, functional two parent household like Demetri did. My uncle took me in and raised me when my mother died from a drug overdose at four years old. I never knew who my father was so my uncle Sir was the only male figure in my life and he wasn't a saint like Demetri's pops. He was one of the few lucky drug dealers who was able to turn his money into a legitimate business. I never knew how much money he was racking up but it must have been a lot for him to put me through private schools, which is where I met Demetri. He never had one woman and he never trusted them. I couldn't count how many times I woke up to a chick with her clothes still in her hands, cursing out my uncle for abruptly putting her out of his house after they finished having sex. He would never let them spend the night and he stressed to me as a young man to never break rule number one: don't catch feelings. He opened up a barbershop to get out of the drug game but he never settled down with one woman. He's still single to this day.

I'd never been in love or had the yearning to respect any woman, and the bitches in college made you think twice about ever trusting a woman. You know how many chicks I had sex with that were in a relationship and claimed to love their partners? There were too many to count and far too many for me to trust any woman. By the way, I don't mean any harm when I refer to women as bitches. What I mean is that there are two different types of women. First, you have the "lady" which is the woman who demands respect because she respects herself and carries herself as such. Then, you got the women who I refer to as bitches, which is exactly as it is. It's a female dog who doesn't care if she's respected or not. She does things that are not lady like with whore tendencies and she's usually ratchet and full of drama. Case in point would be Demetri, he just left the crazy ass bitch Karma and upgraded to a real woman, Kelsey.

When I met Kendra in college, I thought she was cute but I never tried to get with her. I was too busy doing my own thing for me to really pay her any attention. We always flirted with each other though since we were always around one another thanks to Kelsey and Demetri. Plus, she was busy doing her own thing too. She used to have one of those "friends with benefits" agreements with one of my line brothers so technically she was off limits. I finally made it back home. I had a loft style apartment and I couldn't imagine sharing it with a woman. This was my man cave. The only place where I could have a peace of mind without a woman all in my face asking me what was I thinking about every five minutes. I can't lie to myself though, lately I'd been thinking about what it would be like to have a family and a wife. Did I really want to end up like my uncle Sir?

It was getting close to the time Kendra and I had agreed on meeting up, so I started going through my closet to look for something to wear. It wasn't like we were going to an upscale restaurant, so I decided on a navy blue button-up shirt with some blue jeans and my navy blue and white Air Max shoes. As I was getting ready to hop in the shower my phone buzzed and lit up with the text message icon. It was one of my cuddy buddies. She asked if I could come beat it out the frame tonight at her place. She was pissed when I told her I already had a date. She had no reason to be pissed though. She was well aware of her role after she met me so I expected her to play it. Instead of just meeting up at the bowling alley, I decided to pick Kendra up at her place so we could ride together. I looked at myself in the mirror one more time before heading out the door to make my way over to her place. I brushed my waves and sprayed my favorite cologne which was the one that all my bitches seemed to love. A nigga was looking good and I was definitely feeling myself.

It took me about fifteen minutes to make it to Kendra's apartment. Usually, I would just honk my horn or text the chick to let her know I was outside but since Kendra's been demanding respect, I was going to approach her as such with my game face on. I crawled out of my car and buzzed her apartment number, but she opened the door and met me at the entrance. I smiled when I saw how good she looked. All I seen was how nice her ass looked in those leggings. The rest of the outfit didn't even matter. She smiled back at me.

"You smell good, what's the name of that scent?"

"Why? So you can buy it for your man?"

"No, silly I was just making conversation."

"Well in that case it's called *Whitewater Rush* by Bath and Body Works."

"I heard they created a line for men too, but I didn't expect it to smell that good. You probably hear that from all your chicks, though."

"Don't mention other chicks when I'm with you because I know you got niggas on speed dial, so let's just enjoy each other's company."

"I was just kidding, but we can do that."

"You look nice by the way." I said to her.

"Thanks, you look good too."

I opened the passenger door for her and waited for her to climb in. I crawled in behind the wheel and pulled off. The bowling alley wasn't far from her place but of course it was packed considering it was a Saturday night. I paid for our shoes and games while she went over to our assigned lane to get everything set up. I made it over to her and handed over her bowling shoes. She took some socks out of her purse since she was wearing sandals before. I noticed that her feet were actually pretty without a bunion in sight. She was up to bowl first and the entire time I was admiring her ass. She surprised me though when she hit a strike right off the bat. She sashayed over to me with a huge smile on her face.

"You do know that I'm about to whoop your ass, right?"

"I doubt that so don't let that little strike go to your head."

"I'm going to let you know now that I'm very competitive and I don't take loses."

"Well sorry to burst your bubble, but you gone take one today so get prepared for my bragging."

I picked up the green bowling ball and concentrated for a few moments. I got my rhythm going but when I released the ball it instantly hit the gutter and I heard Kendra laughing in the background. The truth is, I'm really not that great at bowling. I just suggested it because I wanted to enjoy the view of her ass while she bowled. She ended up winning all three games and of course she wouldn't stop bragging. It fractured my ego for a second but we decided to play pool for me to redeem myself. She had never played pool before, so I had a good chance of winning. Plus, I had to show her the ropes which I was more than happy to do.

"This game is stupid", she whined.

“It’s not stupid. You’re just mad because you’re not good at it”, I chuckled

“Maybe the teacher I have isn’t that good at showing me how to play.”

“Well, let me teach you a lesson.”

It was her turn to break, so I walked behind her and showed her how to hold the stick. She didn’t resist or protest when my pelvic was practically on her ass. I reached my arm around and placed it over hers. I told her to concentrate on where she wanted to hit the ball because it’s all about angles and strategy. She caught on quick and knocked a striped ball in the pocket. I had to step back away from her because I felt myself getting excited. I played it off by bending down and tying my shoes which were actually already tied. My heart dropped when I stood up to see who was walking towards me.

“So, this is the reason why you couldn’t fuck me Marcus? Is the new bitch the reason why you been acting brand new?” My cuddy buddy Tasha was hovering over me with her arms folded and her eyes squinted in anger.

“Get the fuck out of my face, Tasha. The last time I checked, I was single so don’t come over here with that bullshit like we’re exclusive. Now, go back to wherever you came from so I can enjoy the rest of my date", I explained as I dismissed her emotional outbursts.

"Fuck you, Marcus! Make sure you lose my fucking number because I'm done with your trifling ass!"

"Consider your number already lost. Deuces." I threw up the peace sign to elaborate.

Tasha stormed off while cursing me out and making a scene. Surprisingly, Kendra wasn't fazed by this groupie disrespecting her and calling her every name but the child of God. After that episode, I didn't want to risk running into another crazy ass female so we left the bowling alley and headed back to her place. I pulled into the parking lot and shut off my car. I already knew there was no chance in hell of me getting some pussy tonight after Tasha fucked up my chances but still I walked around and opened her car door for her. She thanked me as we walked up to the entrance of her building. She wished me a good night and was about to walk away when I stopped her.

"I'm sorry about that chick and how she disrespected you. I just want you to know that she doesn't mean anything to me."

"It's cool, Marcus. You don't have to explain yourself", she said as she searched her purse for her keys.

"I know that I don't. I just want to make that clear. I would love to make it up to you though. My frat brother's wife is throwing him an extravagant birthday party next Saturday. I was going to go by myself, but I'd rather go with you." She looked up and smiled at me.

"Sure, it's been awhile since I've been to a party. How should I dress?"

"She always has a theme for his parties. This year it's a masquerade ball and Hollywood glam theme. She does it big every year."

"Well, I'd love to go with you. I wouldn't miss an opportunity to get all dolled up either."

"Cool, I'll pick you up around eight. Make sure you buy a mask and wear something sexy."

I stepped closer to her so much so that my lips were inches away from hers. We stopped talking and looked into each other's eyes. I contemplated on whether or not I should kiss her. I could tell she was wrestling with her thoughts too. Her body and her mind didn't seem to be on the same page. I leaned in and kissed her thinking she was going to reject me but she didn't. She actually kissed me back. Her lips were as soft as pillows and her breath was minty. Her kiss was one of those "I want to rip your clothes off and fuck you right now" types of kisses. My hands were gripping her ass when she pulled away from me. I was disappointed because I might be taking another cold shower. She leaned in close and whispered in my ear with her hand resting on my groin.

"I guarantee that when we go down that road, you'll be addicted so you better watch it."

"Good, I need a drug to be addicted to so why not it be you?" I smirked at her.

"Good-night Marcus. Drive home safe."

"Good-night. I'll talk to you soon."

I was determined more than ever to experience whatever it was Kendra had to offer. I'd never met a woman who constantly rejected my swag and offers of sex. I can't deny that it turned me on and of course it grabbed my attention for her even more. I realized now that I have to do more than put my game face on; I had to actually be prince charming. Usually, I would refrain from actually getting to know a chick, but Kendra wasn't just the average chick. This constant rejection was starting to hurt my ego.

Since we had already exchanged numbers, my plan was to call her more just to let her know I was thinking about her. Maybe I would also randomly send her flowers and try to be more romantic. However, I was lacking in the romance department but I knew Demetri corny ass wasn't so I planned on hitting up my boy later to get a few pointers. This chase was already starting to be too much work, but I planned on going the extra mile this week though because I couldn't go another week without sex. I'd already been dodging my bitches because I was too busy trying to get what I really wanted from Kendra. The plan was to wine and dine her this Saturday and do everything that makes a woman happy leading up to the day of the party. I figured since Demetri was such a sucker for love and I needed some help on the romance thing, I'd called him first.

"What's good bro, are you busy?"

"No, I'm just chilling with Kelsey right now. What's up?"

"You think you can meet me at the Y? I need to chop it up with you and I don't want Kelsey to hear our conversation."

"Are you talking about right now?"

“Yeah, meet me right now nigga. I need some advice on something.”

“Man, you cutting into my alone time with my girl, but since this seem so urgent I’ll be there in thirty minutes.”

“Man, you been with her every day now. An hour apart won’t kill you”, I complained.

“Shut up! I said I’ll be there in thirty minutes. This better be important.”

“It is. It’s a matter of life and death.”

“Alright, I’ll be there.”

Demetri and I usually go to the YMCA and shoot some hoops a couple times a week, but when he’s in a relationship you can only expect him to show up once a week if you’re lucky. I was already in the gym putting some shots up when Demetri walked in. He was in his basketball gear already so he started shooting around with me immediately.

“So, what’s this life and death situation that you claim you’re having?”

“My frat brother is having a masquerade ball party this Saturday. I’m taking Kendra as my date and I wanted to wine and dine her with some romance. I just don’t know how to be romantic.”

"Okay, I understand that but how is this a life and death situation?"

"It's life and death because I haven't had sex in two weeks chasing after her. I would be pulling my hair out right now if I had some." Demetri laughed at that.

"That's hilarious."

"My lack of sex is funny to you?"

"Yeah, it's funny as hell because we switched places. Remember when you laughed at me because I wasn't getting any? It doesn't feel too good, uh?"

"Shut up! This is just a temporary drought, unlike months like you. That's why I need some advice on the romance thing because this drought ends Saturday."

"I should go and bring Kelsey with me as a date, but the romance part is easy. All you have to do is be a gentleman. Don't bring up the topic of sex. I know that part is hard for you but so be it. You have to actually pay attention to her and what she says. To be honest, she already knows you're a man whore so she's probably just waiting on some type of commitment from you", Demetri declared as he missed a free throw.

"I'm just trying to get sex without a commitment. Not make a commitment just to get sex. That's stupid!" I grabbed the rebound and attempted a three pointer.

"It may be stupid to you, but it's not to most women. I can tell that you really like her, especially since you haven't had sex in two weeks and you're single."

I thought about what Demetri just said to me. I knew I liked her, but was I ready to be exclusive with one woman? Was I ready to break rule number one: don't catch feelings? I must admit that she got me putting in time and effort to pursue her because I'm used to bitches constantly sweating me, not rejecting me. She's been on my mind a lot more than I would like to admit. Maybe it was time for me to turn in my player card. I decided I would make my mind up by Saturday before she loses interest in me and moves on to a fuck boy.

"Yeah, you got a point. Would you call me soft if I was catching feelings for her? This shit isn't me; I don't know how to feel about it", I stated as I passed him the ball.

"No, I wouldn't call you soft. I would call you human. You can't control the way you feel about someone, that shit just hits you when you least expect it."

"Yeah, you right about that because just a few weeks ago, I was juggling three women and getting sex on the regular but now I'm damn near celibate!" I cringed at the thought of being celibate for months. That word has never belonged in my vocabulary.

"Dude, I guarantee being celibate for Kendra would be worth it in the end. You just have to be patient."

"Alright, I got one more question and then you can run back to Kelsey. It might be a little personal though."

"Just ask because Kelsey is cooking at her crib so you're about to get left. Besides, it's not like you never asked me anything personal before so why act shy now?" Demetri joked.

"I know you've probably tried oral sex on Kelsey by now, how is it?"

"I'm guessing you never did it before?"

"Fuck no! I'm not putting my tongue anywhere on a chick if she's not exclusively mine", I said with a disgusted mug on my face. My tongue belongs to me and only me until further notice.

"Well, it all depends on you. If you care about your girl and she likes to receive head just like you do, then you learn to love it if you already don't. I like it though."

"Yeah, of course you do", I laughed at him.

"You talking shit now but it looks like you're going to be in the same boat pretty soon. Just care about her being pleasured just as much as you cared about busting a nut and you'll be fine. Told you, you should have taken that anatomy course with me in college but you laughed at that idea. You'll be surprised at what you can learn about a woman's body. But if you'll excuse me I have some food waiting on me to devour so I'll catch up with you later." He gave me dabs then gathered his things to leave.

"Alright, let me know if you and Kelsey are going to the party!" I yelled to him as he was leaving.

"Cool, I'll ask her about it when I see her."

So, I finally decided on how to go about handling this romance thing with Kendra. I arranged for a dozen red roses to be delivered to her job. If you would have asked me about sending a chick flowers before now, I would have clowned you for even letting that thought come to mind. It's funny how that one person can change your perspective on things. I was shocked when I found myself wondering how she would react and hoping that this gesture wouldn't be rejected. Today was Monday, so I was back in my office handling some paperwork when I glanced at the clock and realized it was about time for my flowers to be delivered. I pulled out my cell phone and dialed Kendra's number with a smile on my face.

"Hello?" She sounded so sexy.

"Hey, how's your day going so far?"

"It's going a lot better now that I've seen this pretty bouquet of flowers. To what do I owe this pleasure?"

"Nothing, I was just thinking about you and wanted you to know that, hence the flowers."

"Well, thank you. I appreciate it. I was thinking about you too." I can tell she was smiling on the other end of the phone.

"Really, what were you thinking about?"

"Just thinking about how much I wanted to see you. Too bad I'll be busy all week because of new clients, but I'm looking forward to this party on Saturday."

"Yeah, I'm looking forward to it too. I have a few surprises up my sleeve for you as well."

"Really? I already know you're not going to tell me so I won't waste my time on asking what they are."

"I'm glad you said that because I wasn't going to tell you anyway. It'll be worth the wait though."

"Are you sure about that?"

"Yeah, I'm positive", I said with confidence.

"Okay, we'll see about that. I have an appointment with a client so I'll talk to you later."

"Alright, I'll talk to you soon. Bye."

Since she was going to be busy for the rest of the week, I decided to take this time to get my surprises for the party in order. At first, I was going to stop at sending the flowers, but then I said fuck it! I might as well go big or go home. Instead of either one of us driving to the party, I rented a limo and a chauffeur for the evening. Instead of her buying herself something to wear, I would buy her dress, shoes, jewelry, and mask and have them sent to her house. I know Demetri said not to bring up the topic of sex, but he didn't say anything about buying something that's sexual in nature as a gift. So, I was going to take a big risk by buying Kendra some lingerie and having it sent to her house with the other items as well in hopes that I'll have the pleasure of taking it off later. If all this hard work doesn't pay off, I'm gonna be pissed but I refuse to give up that easily.

The only problem was, I didn't know any of her sizes in clothing or anything about what she personally liked to wear so I called Demetri to get Kelsey's number. I knew her best friend could help me out. Demetri was hesitant about giving me Kelsey's number like I was trying to steal his girl or something. That's what you call being whipped for real. Once he finally gave it to me, I called Kelsey's number and waited for her to answer.

"Dr. Smith speaking, how can I help you?"

"Hey, Kelsey this is Marcus. I was calling to see if you were busy?"

"No, I'm not busy I have some time to spare."

"I need a huge favor from you pertaining to Kendra."

"Sure, what's up?"

"First, I need you to promise me that you won't tell her anything because it's a surprise."

"My word is bond. I promise I'll keep whatever it is to me and me only", she promised.

"Do you know what sizes Kendra wears in shoes, dresses, bras and panties?"

"Yeah, we pretty much wear the same sizes in everything. I can go to the mall with you if you'd like."

"Yeah, that'll be perfect. You know her style better than I do anyways. Are you available to go now?"

"Yeah, my last appointment was cancelled. You can pick me up from office. We're going to work out in a couple hours so now would be the best time to go."

"Alright, I'll be on my way soon."

The first place we went to was *Victoria's Secret*. I didn't realize how expensive bras and panties were until now. I just sat back and let Kelsey pick out everything that she knew Kendra would love. My only request was that whatever she picked out, it had to be all black since that was my favorite color. After that, we went to another store and bought a black fitted strapless gown with silver heels and accessories. I had spent a pretty penny after doing all that ripping and running at the mall but I knew it was going to pay off though. After we left the mall, I dropped Kelsey back off at her office so that she could meet up with Kendra. I was driving back to my place when my phone rang. It was my uncle Sir.

“What’s up Pops I haven’t heard from you in a while. What you been up to?”

“I been at the shop. You could have stopped by anytime. You know where I’m at!” he yelled on the other end of the phone.

“Yeah, that’s my bad. I just been busy with work and all. You know how that goes.”

“Yeah right. You been preoccupied with more than just work. So what’s her name?”

“How do you know this is about a woman?”

“I know because it’s the same reason why you haven’t heard from me in a while. I met a woman that got me breaking all my rules.”

“Wow, I never thought I’d see the day that you would settle down. This love shit must be in the air or something”, I chuckled as I made a right turn.

“Are you in love with this woman?”

“I’m not in love with her yet, but I can see myself being in love with her and I haven’t even had sex with her yet!” I never thought I'd ever say the love word to any woman, but here I was beaming at the thought of it.

"Wow, she must be making you earn the benefits that she has to offer. Sounds like a special woman if you ask me."

"Yeah, that she is. Her name is Kendra and she's pretty much the female version of me; like my other half or something. You might meet her one day."

"I'll be looking forward to it. Look, I have to go, some nappy headed boy just walked in the shop. Just make sure you don't fuck up with your girlfriend."

"Yeah, I hear you Pops. I'll talk to you soon."

Did he just say girlfriend? I hadn't thought about the fact that I hadn't made that commitment just yet, but would I really spend a couple hundred dollars for one night on a woman who wasn't my girlfriend? I guess subconsciously, I had already made that decision. I never had a girlfriend before and honestly, I didn't know how to ask her to be more than just friends. Saturday couldn't come fast enough because I had made up my mind that would be the day that I'd share my feelings with her.

Chapter Seven:

Kendra

Thank goodness it's Friday. I'm glad that business is booming but this week has been hectic and stressful. I was totally looking forward to this party because I needed to enjoy myself after the week I just had. Marcus had been surprising me a lot lately. He was being such a gentleman that it honestly scared me a bit. I wasn't conditioned to really be around a man who was actually a gentleman. I'd been receiving different types of flowers delivered to my job every day, not to mention the good morning texts and midday phone calls. I must admit that he was being really sweet instead of pushing sex so hard. Last Saturday's kiss almost made me give in though and I'm sure he sensed it too. The passion behind his kiss told me that he needed me like his next breath and the feeling was mutual. However, I had to fall back because I felt myself losing control. My plan was to keep the cookies inside the cookie jar until I get a commitment from him because I was tired of the friends with benefits arrangement that usually turned into "situationships" due to someone catching feelings. The person to catch feelings was never me though. I was cold-hearted when it came to loving and trusting but for a good reason. I'm not saying that all men are cheaters and womanizers but a great majority of them are including my own father.

My parents were happily married until the day my mom left work early to pick me up from school because I was sick. She took me home to care for me while my dad was supposedly at work. At the time, I was too young to understand the noises coming from their bedroom but I would never forget the look she had on her face when she heard it. She told me to stay at the front door while she took the trash out. I did as I was told and waited by the front door. I saw my mother take a black object out of her purse while she walked in a daze down the hallway that led to their bedroom. I heard several loud bangs that almost startled me half to death. My heart started pounding as I stood there silently with tears running down my cheeks. My mom soon returned in a rush with a bag of trash in her hands and an emotionless face. Apparently, my father was having an affair with my Aunt Brenda unbeknownst to my mother. She was my favorite aunt because she was always around buying me candy and toys but now as an adult, I understood why she was always around when my mother was at work.

My aunt was instantly killed with a single gunshot wound to the temple. My father had several gunshot wounds though. He was shot in his lower back, his right shoulder, and his penis. He survived his injuries but he was left paralyzed with his manhood blown completely off. After the shootings, my mother took me to my favorite restaurant because she knew our time together would be short lived. I was only seven at the time of the shooting but I'll never forget it or forget what she said to me before she was arrested, "Kendra, this may be the last time you'll ever see me as a free woman. I'm ashamed and I'm already regretting the decisions I made in the heat of the moment. I want you to know that I love you with all my heart and I hope that you'll understand once you become a woman. Do me a favor, please? Don't ever let your emotions get the best of you, especially to the point where you're taken out of character. I love you forever and a day, baby just remember that."

I visited my mother every week while she was incarcerated until she passed away. I always thought she died from a broken heart because there was no other explanation for her death according to her autopsy. Ironically, my dad was still living with his injuries. I never forgave him for disrespecting my mother and tearing our family apart. As far as I was concerned, he was dead to me too. How can you claim to be in love with my mother while having an affair with my aunt? That destroyed me psychologically and emotionally, which is why I avoided relationships like the plague. Marcus was slowly knocking down the walls that I had built to protect myself. However, for the first time in my life, I was actually willing to help someone knock them down with me.

The party was tomorrow night and I was ecstatic to say the least. I had been so busy that I hadn't had the time to go to the mall to find something to wear. I still wanted to get pampered with a spa day though after the week I'd had, I needed it anyway. My spa day included a full body massage, a manicure and pedicure and a trip to the hair salon which would all be completed tomorrow morning. I still needed to go to the mall though so I called Kelsey to see if she would go with me.

"Hello?"

"What's up, girl. You want to go to the mall with me? I need to find something for this party."

"Uh, when are you trying to go?"

"Right now would be a good time because I'm going to be busy tomorrow morning."

"Sorry, Kendra my schedule is booked with appointments that can't be cancelled. The only time I can go with you is tomorrow. I'm sure we can squeeze it in before the party starts."

"You know I hate shopping by myself Kelsey. You sure you can't move an appointment around or something?"

"I'm positive, but I am available tomorrow so just call me when you're done with your spa day so we can go to the mall real quick."

"Alright, just make sure you'll be ready tomorrow. I don't want to rush getting ready for the party."

"I promise that I'll be ready. Just call me."

"Alright, I'll see you later."

It was late when I got off the phone with Kelsey and I was already exhausted from a stressful week so I decided to call it a night. The next morning I woke up to make myself some breakfast and my daily smoothie for the long day I had ahead of me. I got dressed and made my way to the nail salon first. It felt so good to just relax while being pampered. I couldn't decide on which color I wanted to paint my fingernails and toenails. I had pretty much tried every color in the salon except for black, so that's the color that I ended up choosing. After I left the nail shop, I went to my favorite spa to get a massage and bikini wax. Kelsey had always asked me how I took the pain of bikini waxes. I always told her it's temporary pain for weeks of pleasure because I hated shaving every day. Besides, no one likes hair in their food. After I left the spa, my last trip was to get my hair done. I'd never had a relaxer before in my hair because my mother made sure of that, so I'd always been team natural. I decided to simply wear my hair bone straight for the evening. I was finally done ripping and running around 6:30 P.M. when I pulled out my phone to call Kelsey but her phone went straight to voicemail which was unlike her. She always kept her phone charged and on her just in case TJ needed to contact her. I called her again but her phone still went straight to voicemail.

I walked inside my apartment and decided to shower and do my makeup so I could go ahead and get it out of the way. Makeup was really simple for me though. I only used mascara, sometimes eyeliner and eyeshadow or a bold lipstick. I settled for just mascara and a bold lip for the evening. I love eyeliner, but sometimes it left me looking like a raccoon the next morning when it smudged under my eyes. After showering, doing my makeup and moisturizing my skin with my favorite lotion scent, I called Kelsey to see if maybe she had charged her phone by now. It went straight to voicemail again. It was almost 7:15 P.M. and I was about to have a bitch fit until there was a buzz for my apartment number. I thought to myself it must be Kelsey to finally pick me up so we can go shopping. When I opened the door, there was a young black man dressed in a tuxedo with bags and boxes in his hands.

"Are you Miss Kendra?"

"Yeah, that's me. Can I help you?"

"My name is Bobby and I'm your driver for the evening. Your date, Marcus Love has requested for you to accept these gifts, get dressed, and come outside to the limo that will be waiting outside for once you're done", he stated as he handed me the bags and boxes.

"Are you serious?" I looked inside the bags and seen a beautiful black strapless gown, silver shoes, and jewelry to match.

"Yes, he must really like you. I'll be waiting outside when you're ready", he smiled and retreated to wait outside for me.

I peeped inside the second bag that was from *Victoria's Secret*. There was a black strapless bra and a lace thong to go under my dress of course. Then, I took out a black sheer teddy and thong set. I couldn't help but smile from ear to ear at Marcus boldness. I don't know how he knew my size for everything, but it all fit perfectly and he actually had good taste. If he keeps up the good work, I don't know how long I can keep the cookies in the cookie jar. I finally finished getting dressed and looked at myself in the mirror. I definitely looked as if I belonged on the red carpet in this gown. I walked outside to a beautiful, warm summer night. The limo driver was leaning on the passenger door as he waited outside of the car. He opened the back door for me as I approached the car. I was a little disappointed when I noticed the limo was empty. I thought Marcus was going to be inside waiting on me. Instead, there was some wine and a glass, my mask for the ball which was black of course, and a folded note. The note read, "I told you the surprises would be worth the wait. I hope you're enjoying the gifts and the wine so far. I have one more surprise for you that you'll be happy about. I'll see you soon."

I couldn't believe Marcus had gone the extra mile just to impress me. I was flattered that he was putting in this much effort just to make me happy when we didn't even have a title for whatever this was that we were doing. I never had a man treat me the way he'd been treating me and I noticed that my feelings for him were growing deeper. I was still scared of getting hurt but now I was open to the idea of being in love and in a relationship. The driver finally stopped in front of a downtown hotel. One that I had never been to before. Marcus was outside waiting with both hands in his pockets, looking good as hell and sporting his pearly whites. He had on an all-black suit with black oxfords and black shades along with diamond studs in his ears that were very noticeable and a silver watch on his wrist. I could tell he had just got a fresh hair cut for the evening and his smooth brown skin was glowing under the hotel lights. He was exuding sex appeal so effortlessly and it was turning me on to no end. He smiled when the driver opened the door and I stepped out holding my dress, carefully trying not to trip over my gown. I almost stood exactly at his height with these particular heels on. I made eye contact with him and smiled. Damn he was so fine! By now the cookies were damn near spilling out of the jar.

"You look so beautiful. Did you enjoy the surprises?" he asked as flashed me his seemingly perfect smile.

"I did more than enjoy them, I loved them. You look really handsome."

"Come inside, I want to show you off to some of my friends", he smiled at me.

Marcus grabbed me by the hand and led me inside the hotel. The setting was elegant. The lights were dim and everyone was dressed to impress. My eyes lit up when I see Kelsey and Demetri dancing together. I snuck up behind Kelsey and tapped her on her shoulder.

"Was there a reason for you to be ignoring my calls Dr. Smith?" I asked with my head tilted to the side.

"I'm sorry. I just didn't want to ruin the surprise. You look good though! You two look good together", she smiled.

"Don't compliment me when I'm trying to be mad at you! I'm glad you didn't ruin the surprise though, I wasn't expecting this at all", I blushed.

"Yeah I know. I'm glad you like the dress that I picked out."

"So, he recruited you to help impress me? That's so sweet."

"Yeah he surprised me too, but here comes your boo."

Marcus walked behind me and wrapped his arms around my waist. I wasn't used to public affection but his strong arms surrounding me made me feel comfortable and at ease. He took me around the party and introduced me to his friends and frat brothers. However, he did something that I didn't expect when he introduced me to the birthday boy. We walked hand-in-hand to a beautiful couple who was seated in the VIP section. The guy stood and embraced Marcus. His wife was dressed in a red strapless gown with her hair in an up-do style and she was absolutely gorgeous.

"Kendra, this is my frat brother and my homeboy Derek. Dereck, this is my girlfriend Kendra. And this is his wife, Lisa. She's the one responsible for this extravagant party", he said as Lisa stood to hug him as well.

Excuse me? Did he just call me his girlfriend? I'm guessing this was the last surprise that he was speaking of. The cookies were fully out the jar now! He was in for a special treat whenever we got some alone time.

"Nice to finally meet you Kendra. I've been hearing a lot about you lately. You must be something special to tame this guy", Derek smiled as he kissed my hand.

“Nice to meet you as well. This party is a great turn out by the way.” I said as I turned my attention to Lisa.

“Thank you. My wife is an event planner so she does it big every year”, he declared as he took a seat next to Lisa.

“We’ll leave you two lovebirds alone so I can steal a dance with my girl. I’ll catch up with you later bro”, said Marcus.

Marcus grabbed me by the hand again and led me to the middle of the dance floor where Kelsey and Demetri were. There was a slow jam playing when he pulled me closer to him and wrapped his arms around my waist again. His hands dropped from my waist to my hips as I slowly grinded my ass on his pelvis. I felt his dick hardening like the night we played pool only, this time he didn’t try to play it off. We pretty much stayed on the dance floor for the remainder of the evening. I was glad we had a limo because we both were more than tipsy when we finally left the party.

We were all over each other in the limo on the ride back to my apartment. We were waiting outside of my door while I was trying to find my keys in my purse in the midst of him groping me. I barely turned the key when we finally stumbled inside. Before I could even sit my purse down, he pushed me up against the wall and positioned my hands above my head. He slowly unzipped the back of my dress and it fell around my ankles. With my hands still pinned to the wall, he looked me up and down to see the matching bra and panty set that he had bought. He looked at me as if he wanted to put me on a platter and devour me as I bit down on my lower lip and let him enjoy the view. He kissed my neck and whispered in my ear.

"Do you want me to fuck you or make love to you?"

"I want you to fuck me", I responded as I bit down on my lower lip again.

"Take this off and put on the lingerie I bought you but keep the heels on", Marcus demanded as he loosened his tie and retreated to my bedroom without saying another word.

I did as I was instructed and went to the bathroom to put on the lingerie and freshen up. Usually, I'm the person who calls the shots, not the other way around but Marcus being in charge was sexier than I expected it to be. It was still going to be hard not being in control during sex. For me, sex was just as enjoyable as working out and I wasn't lazy at it either. I lightly sprayed some perfume on my skin and checked out myself in the mirror before meeting Marcus in the bedroom. He was lying on top of the sheets with his hands positioned behind his head and legs spread wide with only his briefs on. I slowly strutted in with my heels and lingerie on as he demanded. I was about to climb on the bed when he stopped me.

“Wait. Stand right there and slowly turn around so I can admire every inch of you”, he commanded.

Once again I did as I was instructed and slowly turned around so he could enjoy the view. There was nothing shy about me when it came to sex, especially when it came down to showing off my body because it was in damn good shape and I was completely comfortable in my skin. Looking at Marcus’ damn near naked body in front of me, I could tell that his physique was far from mediocre as well. I must admit that I was a little nervous about this because I wasn’t used to foreplay or making love and so far, it seemed as if Marcus wanted to take his time. This was definitely going to take some getting used too.

“Take the lingerie off for me”, he instructed with authority in his tone.

I made eye contact with him the entire time as I pulled my panties down and slipped the teddy of my shoulders and let it fall to the floor. His eyes were glossy and filled with lust. He was rubbing his dick and staring at me when he motioned for me to come to him with his finger. I climbed on top of him completely naked with my heels still on as requested. He lifted his head to give me a kiss and I felt him growing harder underneath me while he griped my ass with his massive hands.. I was astonished when he lifted me and positioned me to sit on his face. This was a first for me because oral sex was an intimate act reserved for couples in my opinion so I was never really interested in it, but the way his tongue was circling my clit had me in pure bliss. I moaned and caressed the waves in his hair. I was loving everything that he was doing to me so I felt the urge to please him the same way he was pleasing me. I turned around to get into the 69 position and pulled his briefs down while he continued pleasuring me. I had never gave head before so this would be a new experience for me, but based off what I heard from Kelsey, it's not hard at all especially if you enjoy it. A part of me always thought it was disgusting but it’s funny how things can change under the right circumstances.

Giving him head was something that I found myself enjoying. I had never tried it before I watched enough X-rated movies to know what to do. I had enough of the foreplay though; I wanted to feel him inside of me like something serious. I was already on top so I positioned myself with my back towards him in the reverse cowgirl position, which has always been my personal favorite. I grabbed a condom from my nightstand and ripped it open. I always protected myself and being with Marcus wasn't an exception. He would also be asked to take an STD screening just like my previous partners were. I rolled the condom onto his dick and climbed back on top. This was my favorite position because for one, I was a complete control freak and two, I know where my "G" spot is better than most men do. Sadly, unlike them I can hit it every time.

Typically, I would get into my favorite position, do my thing, and get an orgasm and get dressed and leave, whether got theirs or not. I guess you could call that cold-hearted or inconsiderate? Unfortunately, men do it all the damn time but its cold-hearted when women do it? An adventurous woman, such as myself, I hated those types of double standards. I must have been in the zone while I was on top because Marcus caught me off guard and surprised when he suddenly flipped me over to my knees. I guess the slow lovey-dovey wasn't in his nature either. He grabbed a handful of my hair and jerked my head back while whispering in my ear.

"Since it seem like you want yo brains fucked out that's what I'm going to do." His grip on my hair grew tighter which excited me.

I was out of my element when he took control. This was definitely going to take some getting used to but I have to admit that he didn't have a hard time finding my spot. I'll give him his props. He knew what he was doing when it came to sex. He was hitting my spot from behind and pulling my hair at the same time. I couldn't lie, there was just something about rough sex that turned me out and right off the bat, I noticed Marcus was a shit talker during sex with his arrogant self. I think I've met my match!

I came two times when he decided to change positions with me being back on top. Only this time, I was facing him. This amazingly had me acting all shy. It was the way he kept looking at me as if he could see straight through me. I know I told him I was just trying to fuck, but the look in his eyes was more than just lust. Lust was a look I'd seen many times before. That was the look of love brewing in his eyes so I decided to change my approach and take my time to relish every minute of riding him. His hands were gripping my hips while I rocked his body back and forth. He moaned when I reached my hand under myself to massage his balls. He leaned forward and put my nipple in his mouth, slowly swirling his tongue around the ring before nibbling on it. These sensations were a first for me and it had my head spinning. I found myself moaning his name while he lightly nibbled on my breast and gripped my ass so he could enter inside me as deep as possible. I was reaching yet another orgasm when he let go of my breast and laid his head back on my pillow. He held my hands and continued the rhythm of me rocking his body back and forth, meeting my tempo thrust for thrust.

"I want to hear you say my name when you come." Marcus whispered in between moans and strokes.

"Can you hush cause you messing up the vibe", I told him. He was getting in the way of my climax.

"I can stop hitting that spot if that's what you want, now say my name." His arrogance was such a turn on.

"Just don't stop", I moaned as I continued riding him. He was literally driving me crazy.

"I told you to say my name."

He was still gripping my hips and thrusting his hips to meet my motions but at a much slower pace. He was still hitting my spot though. Remarkably I loved the slow, deliberate strokes instead of the fast pace at the moment. I damn sure wasn't going to say his name now since I was enjoying the ride too much. His strokes were still at a slow pace but they were long and penetrating. I was already reaching a climax, but when he started rubbing my clit while slow stroking me, my body lost all control. My legs were riddled with vibration when my juices were released like the floodgates being opened. I'm pretty sure he was happy that he got what he wanted when I moaned his name over and over. I was experiencing waves of pleasure from aftershock, which had never happened to me before. Shortly after my orgasm, his body stiffened and his thrusts came to a halt as he bit down on his lip and enjoyed the after effects of busting a nut. I remained on top of him and caught my breath as he caressed my breast and lips and kissed my body all over. I took a moment to actually look into his pretty, light brown eyes. From his brown skin to his white teeth and fresh haircut, everything just screamed sex appeal. He returned my gaze and it made me a bit uncomfortable because his stare was intimidating yet intriguing at the same time. He raised his hand and stroked my cheek with the back of his hand. His eyes didn't waver from mine when I leaned in and kissed him. I felt him hardening inside of me again. He changed the condom and laid me on my back to take control once more. I usually hated this position because it allowed little movement. Plus, it was just simply boring and lazy, or so I thought. He crawled in between my legs and slowly slid the tip inside of me. His eyes connected with mine even in the dark as I bit down on my lower lip. He kissed my lips and suppressed the moans escaping from me. Once again, his strokes were slow and deliberate. I raised my hips to meet his thrusts all while contracting my walls. I enjoyed the moans coming from him. It was sexy as hell.

Marcus pushed both of my legs behind my head which wasn't an issue for me considering that I'd always been flexible. He maneuvered his way in and out of me with a vengeance and soon quickened his pace while pushing my legs back as far as they could go. I was in heaven and based off the scrunched up look on his face, he was somewhere between heaven and paradise. I reached down and massaged his balls once more. He moaned some curse words and bit down on his lower lip before climaxing. We stayed in that position for a while and caught our breaths. He kissed me on my lips again, and then went inside my bathroom. I couldn't help but think about the events that had just occurred. I see what Kelsey was talking about when it came to making love. I still love rough sex, but I wouldn't knock making love anymore. However, now that the cookies were clearly out of the jar, I was curious to know where Marcus wanted to go with this though. A part of me wanted him to spend the night so I could actually experience what cuddling and sleeping with someone is like but I wasn't going to force the issue. He returned from my bathroom with a grin on his face. He went to his pile of clothes and pulled his phone out of his pocket. Unexpectedly, instead of putting his phone back in his pocket, he placed it on my night stand and climbed in bed next to me. He laughed at me when he caught me gawking at him.

"Why are you staring at me so hard?"

"You just been full of surprises lately. What's gotten into you?"

"What? A man can't show his woman that he genuinely adore her without being questioned?"

"You're not just any man, Marcus. Let us not forget your track record with women, so excuse me if I'm being offensive but in your case questions are necessary."

"Please don't sit here and judge me as if you don't have a past. My track record with women is exactly what it is; it's the past because I want to build a relationship with you so don't let my past deter you from building with me. We both have our issues, we're both broken and we should be fixing each other for the better. You're just going to have to trust me like I'm putting my trust in you."

I looked into his eyes to see if he really meant what he was saying to me since the eyes are the window to the soul. Something told me that his expression and his words were sincere. He made a valid point too. If we wanted to truly build with one another, I was going to have to put the past in the past and fully trust him. Well, I guess here goes nothing.

“You’re right, and I’m sorry. I do have trust issues but I’m willing to put the past behind us and trust you.”

“Just give me the opportunity to show you that all men aren’t dogs and that a man can actually change his ways. That’s all I’m asking for. We can take things slow if that’s the way you want to go about it. Just give me 100% of you and I’ll give you all of me in return. Can we do that?”

“Yeah, we can do that”, I smiled at him.

“So, since we’ve got that out of the way, I should officially ask you this question. Will you be my girlfriend?” he smiled back.

“Of course I will be your girlfriend.” I was smiling too damn hard now.

“Can I spend the night with you?”

“I would love for you to spend the night with me Marcus.” He must’ve been reading my mind.

"One last question, do you want to take a shower with me?"

"You already know the answer to that question. Let me get my clothes together, and then I'll meet you there." I was about to get up to gather my clothes until he stopped me.

"Trust me when I say you won't be needing any clothes." he smirked at me.

Marcus grabbed me by the hand and led me to the bathroom. We enjoyed taking a shower together and being goofy with one another. I never realized how funny he was until now. He had a sense of humor that I never really appreciated before because I was unable to see past his womanizing ways. A man with the ability to make a woman laugh constantly was such a plus! I could see myself falling for him hard and for once in my life, I was okay with that. After showering, we cuddled and talked about our childhood memories. I was taken aback when he told me about the bad times of his childhood, but it gave me a better understanding of why he didn't trust women. After sharing his childhood with me, I felt compelled to share mines with him. He was astounded by my childhood as well, but he told me how he understood why I was never the relationship type and how he was going to be the man to change that.

I'm sure I drifted off to sleep in the midst of our conversation because I don't even remember falling asleep. This week has really drained me.

I made breakfast for us the next morning. After we finished eating, we lounged around my apartment until I brought out my game systems. He was shocked to see that I was a video game fanatic just as much as he was. I was more so a fan of the classic game systems, like *Nintendo 64* and *Sega Genesis* but I still had the latest models of *XBOX* and *PlayStation* too. I didn't want to brag, but I had one hell of a game collection as well, so we spent most of the day playing video games and fucking on and off. We ended up not leaving my apartment for the entire weekend. We ordered food, watched movies, played video games, and fucked all over my apartment. I loved the laid back vibe between us. We had more of a homie-lover-friend type of relationship that was so effortlessly between us. We obviously had more in common than we realized. Unfortunately, Monday was right around the corner, so we both had to end our weekend and snap back into reality.

I was met with another beautiful bouquet of flowers when I made it to work. He was really being quite the romantic which was funny because I wouldn't consider myself a sucker for romance. I was a little rougher around the edges. One thing I noticed about Marcus was that his sex drive was high as hell and mine was a reflection of his. We had been texting each other constantly since he'd been at work. He complained to me about how bored he was so me naturally being the flirt that I was asked if I could come bring some excitement to his day. He knew exactly what I meant. I wanted some midday sex and I wanted to do it right there in his office because there was something thrilling about possibly getting caught having sex in an unethical and public place. I had about an hour and a half until my next training session with another client, so I called Marcus to see what he was up to.

"What's up baby?" he answered on the third ring.

"Hey, I got some free time and was wondering if you wanted me to bring you something to eat?" I smiled at the double meaning.

"Yeah, I'm down for that. I was actually about to leave for lunch anyway. What do you have in mind?" he replied, still unaware of my intentions.

"I was just going to bring you something to eat so that we could have lunch in your office if that's cool?"

"Yeah, that's cool. I'll be going on lunch in about thirty minutes."

"Okay, I'll be there soon."

He sent me directions to his job and instructions on where to go once inside the building. I had about thirty minutes to go to the mall and buy some lingerie and a trench coat because the only thing I planned on bringing for lunch was me. I decided on a black lace bra and panties set since he seemed to be obsessed with the color black. I also bought some black leather knee high boots since I was currently wearing tennis shoes. I made it to his job and pulled into the parking lot. I grabbed my favorite red matte lipstick out of my purse and applied it on my lips before lightly spraying my favorite perfume. I glanced at myself in the mirror one more time and I was sexy as hell.

After entering the building, the receptionist informed Marcus of my arrival and gave me the green light to proceed to his office. When I entered his office, he was on the phone so I paticntly waited and took a seat on his desk with my legs crossed. He ended his phone call, but his eyes were glued on his computer screen. He still hadn't noticed my attire so I stood and seductively strutted to the front of his desk. I unbuttoned my trench coat to expose to him what I really meant when I said I was bringing him something to eat but his eyes was stilled glued to his computer screen.

“So what did you bring me to eat?” he asked as he typed away on his keyboard.

“Well, if you would take a second to look at me, you’ll see what I brought you to eat.” He did a double take from his computer screen then to me. He smiled and leaned back in his chair and bit his lip as his eyes looked me up and down.

“Damn! If this meal looks this good, I wonder how it tastes.” he flirted with me and continued to play my game.

“I don't know. It’s been hot and ready for your taking. Maybe you should taste it to see how good it is?” I said as I sat on his desk.

His eyes lit up as he appreciated the fact that I was practically naked on his desk with my legs wide open for his invitation and he instantly bit down on his lower lip. “Damn, Kendra,” were the only words he could muster up before I undid his pants and pulled his dick out and wrapped my lips around it. I only had about forty-five minutes before I had to meet my next client back at the gym so I was expecting this sex session to be a quickie.

I was enjoying my new fetish and I could tell he was enjoying my head game skills as well. I sat back on his desk and was now lying on my back when he took his shirt off and sucked on my nipples. He proceeded to finger me and give me some bomb ass head but I was crunched for time so we would have to save the foreplay for later. He turned me around and bent me over his desk. I wasn't in the mood for the slow lovey-dovey love making this time, I just wanted some raunchy, hardcore and hair pulling sex. I propped my right leg up on his desk and poked my ass in the air. He entered me and smacked my ass which was just fine with me because I'm a fan of pain and pleasure anyway. I was in ecstasy and I hoped the smacking sounds couldn't be heard by his colleagues but at this point I didn't even care because I was close to my climax. Marcus was still pulling my hair and smacking my ass in between strokes and I was about to disturb this entire office with my moans and screams from my orgasm until he covered my mouth with his hand which I ended up biting down on by accident. He came shortly after me and slumped over me while he caught his breath. I hated to confess this but Marcus definitely had me addicted to his sex which was sad because I had never met a man that had me sprung over his dick. I already knew that I was in trouble. He kissed the nape of my neck which sent a tingling sensation throughout my entire body. I wanted another round but I had to run back to work to meet my client. He pulled his dick out and smirked at me while he removed the condom and threw it in the trash can next to his desk. I was smiling hard as hell too, and probably glowing from the good sex we just had.

"Bringing me something to eat huh? I enjoyed the meal, but I still need some real food", he laughed at me.

"Well, to be technical I did indeed bring you something to eat! I knew you were still going to be hungry though so I left the food in my car. Put your shirt on so you can come get it", I said as I searched for my panties.

"I hope you got a comb or something to fix your hair." I took my comb and a compact mirror out of my purse and fixed my hair while he found my panties and handed them to me.

He unlocked the door to his office and opened it for me. The receptionist gave us a knowing look as if she knew what we were just doing behind closed doors. We returned her smile and scurried out of the building. I gave him his food and a kiss on the lips when we reached my car. We made eye contact with each other and I felt like I got lost in his pretty brown eyes.

"That was just an appetizer earlier. I want the full course meal tonight", he proclaimed.

“Anytime, anyplace. I don't care who's around”, I snapped my fingers as I tried my best to imitate Janet Jackson’s “Anytime, Anyplace” song. He laughed at my impersonation and reached in his pocket to pull out a key.

“So, I had this key made for you. It’s the key to my place but it’s more symbolic than that because it’s more like the key to my heart. I know this probably sounds a little corny, but that’s how you got me feeling. Use this key to get into my place tonight and have it ready for me.” He kissed me, and then went back inside the building.

This gesture was a welcomed surprise because I didn’t expect him to get so serious so soon, but honestly we were both at the age where we should be settling down and possibly starting a family. I got a feeling that a proposal was next on his list, but I didn’t want to get my hopes up by assuming. I could tell he was falling hard for me though. After I left work for the day, I went home and packed an overnight bag assuming that I was staying the night at his place. I followed the directions he gave to get to his house and I was utterly shocked when I entered his loft. Besides the fact that it was very clean and seemed to not have a thing out of place, it was decorated nicely and of course everything was practically black including both his living room and bedroom set. I had beat him home since he went to play basketball with Demetri after work. I was going to be waiting butt-ass naked on the couch for him when he got home so that we could fuck in every room.

Chapter Eight:

Tristan

I was more than pissed when my mama introduced me to her so called friend. I wasn't sure if I even like this dude but it didn't matter if I did or not because he wasn't my dad and he would never amount to the man my pops was. I wanted to knock him out right then and there but the scouts were watching my every move, so that wouldn't have been a smart tactic on my part. I'd been the man of the house ever since I was six years old and my mother had never placed these responsibilities on my shoulders. My father's legacy and parenting philosophy made me step up to the plate. He wasn't a deadbeat father by any means and he taught me things in those six years that grown ass men in their thirties and forties still couldn't comprehend. He taught me early on to think with my brain and not with my dick like most black men in society, which was the reason as to why I was still a virgin. Of course the chicks at my school were on my dick but I was too articulate to know that these chicks only viewed me as a mil ticket. They just wanted to ride my coattails in hopes of a better life.

Saying that I was overprotective of my mother was an understatement. I did my research on Mr. Latimore shortly after we met to see if I could find any dirt on him so he could get his ass back out of the picture. Unfortunately, he was as clean cut as they come. As he stated before, he didn't have any illegitimate kids, he was a lawyer with his own practice, and came from a well-educated and financially secure family. He was damn near perfect on paper. I could see why my mother was attracted to him but he still wasn't my dad. It may have been selfish of me not to want my mama to date but I had good reason for her not to. I was there and witnessed her unravel almost to the point of self-destruction when my father was killed. I didn't ever want to see her hit rock bottom again and I don't think her heart could fathom anymore heartbreak. I understood that she was probably lonely and needed some male companionship, but that didn't stop me from being leery of her dating.

I was at school and on my way to gym class when this chick jumped into my path to get my attention. She was cute, but she was too desperate for any dude's attention and she wasn't my type anyway. I had on my headphones listening to music when I had to remove them to hear what she was saying.

"Did you hear what I just said to you Tristan?"

"Obviously I didn't hear you if I had my headphones in." I had a short fuse for people who lacked common sense.

"Well, I just thought I'd be the first to let you know that there's a rumor spreading like wildfire around the school about you", she proudly stated with her neck bobbing from side to side and her arms folded across her chest.

"So what's the rumor you been hearing?" I honestly didn't care about the rumor. I just wanted her to shut up and move around before she made me late to my class. Rumors were for immature people and I'm too mature for that shit.

"Well, word around the school is that you gay as all outside. Is that why you ain't trying to fuck with me? Come to think of it, that may be the only explanation to pass up on this good good."

My adrenaline immediately started rushing through my veins. My heartbeat increased and my fists balled up. All of those anger management tactics my mama taught me flew out the fucking window.

“Who the fuck did you hear that from?”

“Your best friend Anthony told me earlier. I don’t hear you denying it so it must be true”, she announced it as more of a statement rather than a question which only pissed me off even more.

“Let me tell you something, I don’t want to fuck with you because everybody and they mama done been inside that loose ass pussy that you claim is ‘good good’. It’s more like ‘whack whack,’ and I refuse to swap dicks with half of the niggas at this school. Now get the fuck out my face”, I said as I brushed passed her.

She stormed off while talking shit in the process. Moral of the story is don’t disrespect me and I won’t disrespect you. It’s that simple. This Anthony character was far from my best friend. This scrub was more like my arch enemy. This nigga wanted to be me so bad and he wanted my spot as the basketball team captain. He wanted the scouts and scholarship offers that I had in my pocket, the bitches that rode my dick, and the car I whipped while his broke ass was on the bus. I’ll be seeing his hating ass in gym class shortly, so bets believe I got something for him.

All I seen was red when I entered the boys’ locker room to change for class. I was really trying to calm down and relax but that rumor really pissed me off. People didn't understand the presence of peer pressure. It's a shame that dudes in my generation thought you were gay for simply abstaining from sex until marriage. In my parent's days, it was perceived as tradition to abstain from sex. At times, I was convinced that I was born in the wrong generation. The fact that this weak ass chick assumed I was gay solely because I didn't want to fuck her only added fuel to the fire. I couldn't wait to run into Anthony to see if this was really true. I sat in the gym bleachers waiting on the teacher to arrive when Anthony walked in with another player on our team. My heart rate increased again adrenaline started pumping through my veins fueling me for this well overdue altercation. I hopped off the bleachers and approached him.

"What's this I hear about you spreading rumors like a straight female?" I stood in front him ready to throw some hands if he were to respond with an answer I didn't like.

"I'm pretty sure it's not a rumor. If you don't fuck with females, then you clearly gay nigga!"

"What the fuck did you just say?" I asked as I pulled my pants up.

"I said you gay nigga and if yo pops…"

Before he could even finish his sentence, I was on his ass like white on rice. I was going to try and handle this situation like an adult, until he brought my pops into the equation. I hit his jaw as hard as I could with a right hook and knocked him out. I was on his ass before he even had a chance to hit the floor. I lit him up with some face and body shots before eventually busting his nose. I was hovering over him while pummeling his face and body when the security guards finally arrived and intervened, suddenly yanking me off of him. My adrenaline was still pumping when I hauled off and hit one of the guards in his right eye. My anger had gotten the best of me yet again. In my mind, I wasn't just angry with Anthony for spreading rumors or security for breaking up the fight. I was angry with my Heavenly Father for taking my pops away when I needed him most. I was dragged to the principal's office in handcuffs since I was still throwing blows to anyone who even touched me. The principal entered his office with a look of disappointment sketched across his face. He knew my father well. They actually went to this same high school and played basketball together so of course he expected more from me.

"Tristan, I expect you to visit my office during the anniversary of your father's death, but not now. What's the problem?"

"I don't have a problem, okay?" I claimed as I cracked my knuckles.

"I think the blood on your knuckles and clothes indicates more than nothing. So what happened?"

"Anthony on the team is spreading false rumors about me being gay, which I was going to let go until he brought my dad's name up. That's when I went ballistic."

"I understand that you're still dealing with your father's death Tristan, and trust me when I say I lost a good friend too but you can't go through life being angry and beating up anybody who mentions his name. Are you trying to throw all of your scholarships away because that's what's going to happen if you keep up this attitude?"

"No, that's the last thing that I want. You're right, so I'm going to learn how to handle my anger better."

"Well, that's good to hear. I called your mother and informed her of the recent events and she wasn't pleased to say the least."

"Yeah I already know. She hates it when I get into these altercations."

"I'm not going to suspend you this time but don't make me regret my decision. I want you to take the remainder of the day off. Your mother should be on her way soon."

"Thanks, I really do appreciate this", I said as I stood and headed for my locker.

I was finally free from the handcuffs and collecting my books from my locker to complete my homework assignments when my phone rang. It was my mother.

"Hello?"

"So what's the reason you're fighting for this time? What did I tell you about controlling your anger Tristan? Are you trying to lose everything you've worked so hard for, over something that I'm sure was petty?" She was clearly irritated with me.

"He disrespected me by spreading rumors that I'm gay and on top of that he tried to bring pops into this, so that's when I lost it. It won't happen again though."

"I really hope it won't. Your car is still at the shop getting a routine checkup but it'll be ready for pick up later. I won't be able to get you right now because I'm at a doctor's appointment so I'm sending Demetri to pick you up instead. Before you even open your mouth to say something, do me a favor and keep your comments to yourself. He's going to be around from now on so get used to it and I'll see you later. Love you."

"Love you too."

This was just what I needed on top of an already shitty day. I was in no mood to ride around the city with my mom's new "boy toy". I would have taken the city bus if I had some cash on me, but I forgot my wallet in my room this morning. Today was just not my day. I walked through the double doors of our building and seen Mr. Latimore already waiting outside in a nice ass, all white *Range Rover* truck. I was taking my precious time getting to his truck because I didn't want to ride with him anyway. I heard him unlock the doors as I approached him. He was smiling too damn hard for my liking as I climbed in and put my seatbelt on. I didn't even acknowledge him once I got all settled in.

"I heard you had one hell of a day at school, but from the looks of it, you won the fight", he laughed but I didn't respond and I refused to give him any conversation.

"It's obvious that you have some anger issues that need to be handled before they affect you in more ways than one." He continued this one-sided conversation with his eyes on the road.

"I get it. You don't want to communicate with me so I'm taking you to a place where my dad took me when I needed to relieve some stress."

I continued ignoring his advances at communicating until we pulled up to what appeared to be an abandon building. This certainly peaked my interest for sure.

"What exactly is this?" I asked curiously.

"This is the boxing gym that my pops used to bring me to when I was around your age. If you need to beat up on something, the punching bag is the perfect stress reliever", he said as he took the keys out of the ignition and grabbed a bag from the backseat of his truck.

I was still hesitant about entering this run down building, but I really didn't have much of a choice at this point. I was astonished at how decked out and professional it was on the inside. The vibe was pretty laid-back with a few boxers training in the ring, and some classic hip hop music was playing throughout the gym. Mr. Latimore went to the locker to change out of his suit before returning to the main floor where all the action was. He laced me with boxing gloves and settled for a punching bag in the corner. He gave me a few pointers on how to hit the bag without injuring myself and where to hit it. I started punching the bag and immediately began to feel a sense of relief after a few blows. He was trying to motivate me while I was punching the bag as if he was an actual trainer. I'm not gonna lie, after a while I was feeling like I could beat anyone who stepped in the ring with me. The session was going well until he started asking me questions that had me thinking, and I didn't expect what was about to happen when he started probing me.

"Who are you angry with Tristan?"

"Why do you want to know?" I asked as I continued hitting the bag.

"I want to know so that I can help you with your anger issues", he claimed as he held the bag in place for me.

"I don't need your help."

"Answer the question Tristan. Tell me who you're angry with and why while hitting this bag as hard as you can. Trust me it works."

I thought about if for a second and concluded that it didn't hurt to try. It couldn't be any worse than my mother's boring strategies, so naturally my angry rant started off with Anthony of course.

"You not gone snitch to my mama if I start cursing are you?"

"No. It's not like you're eight years old or something. I'm pretty sure she knows that you might curse like a sailor so just do you and let it all out."

"I don't feel sorry for whooping Anthony's ass. He shouldn't dish shit out that he can't handle in return. How stupid could you be though? You're too busy worried about what I'm driving and who I'm fucking when you got the one thing that I can't ever get back. I'll give all this shit up to get my pops back. Why did God have to take my pops, man?" I felt my voice trembling as anger began to boil inside of me. This was the type of anger that forced tears to relentlessly stream down your face with no regard.

I was hitting the bag with every ounce of strength that I had in me until I finally broke down and cried. I never showed emotion, it was a sign of weakness in my opinion, but I couldn't control it this time. This time I couldn't just suck it up and be a man. It felt as if all the anger and frustrations that had been bottling up since I was six years old were released off my chest. I still felt like less of a man by being so emotional in front of others, let alone my mom's new boo and the fact that he was staring at me made it even more awkward.

"Do you have to stare at me like that?"

"Look, I can't say that I know how you feel because I don't, and I know for a fact that I wouldn't be the man that I am today if it wasn't for my pops. This is why young men need father figures. Your mother is an excellent parent, but she can't raise a man to be a man. That's a man's responsibility. I'm not trying to replace your dad, but if you need a father figure I can be that."

"Thanks, I really do appreciate that. Can I ask you a question?"

"Yeah, what's up?" he answered as he took a seat on the bench in the locker room.

"Do you love her?"

"Yes, I do. More than words can explain", he stated confidently.

"And you know this just after a couple of weeks?"

"I've known her for far more than just a couple of weeks, and you can't really put a time frame on love. It doesn't work that way."

"So if you love her so much what's the next step?"

"Don't tell her this, but I've already been shopping for wedding rings. I was just waiting on you to get on board."

"Well as long as she's happy, I'm happy."

"So, does that mean that you're on board?"

"Yeah, I'm on board. I mean she could be dating someone that's a pimp or a drug dealer. I guess things could be worst."

"Yeah, you got a point. Now I just have to figure out how I want to propose."

"I can help you with that. I have an idea for you", I know what makes my mama happy anyway, I thought to myself.

"What do you have in mind?" he inquired

I told Demetri about my idea on how to propose to my mother and he loved it. I eventually put my pride aside and apologized for my rude behavior. He made it hard for me not to respect him because he reminded me of my father in some ways even though I would never tell him that. From now on, my mother doesn't have to worry about me being so angry and fighting anymore. We left the gym and went to the mall to pick out the wedding rings. I was actually enjoying being around an older male who I could learn from and who had more experience with life in general. After we got the rings, we headed back to the house where my mom was but she was already sleeping. This was unusual for her to be asleep so early. I assumed that she must have had a stressful day at work and I know I didn't make it any better with my fight at school. She would normally have dinner ready, but she was knocked out on the couch and still fully dressed. I made some sandwiches and grabbed some chips for us to snack on while we bonded in my own personal man cave. We played *Call of Duty* and chopped it up while my mother slept in the living room. I was surprised to see that we had a lot of similar views on life in general. I was excited about the future for our new family.

Chapter Nine:

Kelsey

I had been feeling horrible these past few days. I had recently picked up a heavier case load due to one of my employees being out for maternity leave and my body wasn't agreeing with it lately. I'd been feeling really dehydrated and fatigued as of late, so I scheduled a doctor's appointment for my annual checkup. I dreaded getting out of my comfortable bed on the day of my appointment. I was getting ready for the appointment when I received a phone call from Tristan's school letting me know that he was involved in yet another fight. I couldn't reschedule the appointment and I didn't have the energy to tackle this issue so I asked Demetri if he could pick up TJ with hopes that they would finally indulge in some male bonding. I really didn't even feel like getting dressed so I threw on a hoodie, leggings, and UGG boots. Besides, it was chilly outside anyway and this was my lazy day attire. I finally made it to the doctor's office and was sitting in the appointment room as I waited for the doctor to return with my annual test results. She conducted an STD screening, blood test, and cervical exam. These were the standard tests and I wasn't nervous at all about any of my results. After a few minutes, she knocked on the door and entered.

"So, Dr. Smith I finally have the results from your entire test this morning. The STD screening came back all negative and your cervical exam was normal. Now, I have an explanation as to why you've been dehydrated and fatigued. Based off your blood work test and your last menstrual cycle you are about two weeks pregnant. Congratulations on the bundle of joy", she smiled from ear to ear.

When I heard pregnancy was the reason I'd been feeling atrocious, I didn't know whether to celebrate or cry my eyes out. I already knew that Demetri want kids, but sometimes men can change for the worst when a baby is actually going to be brought into this world. I decided to keep the news to myself until I could fully digest it. I couldn't tell Kendra because I'm sure she'll spill the beans to Marcus during their pillow talk and I couldn't risk Demetri finding out that way. At the same time I didn't want to bring a child into this world out of wedlock so I was hoping that marriage was in the near future for us but I also didn't want to pressure Demetri. After leaving the appointment, I went to the pharmacy to pick up some prenatal vitamins before going back home to change clothes and get myself ready for work as if nothing had changed. I was so drained by the end of the day that I forgot to check up on Tristan's and Demetri outing together to see how it went and before I knew it, I had already passed out on the couch as soon as I made it home.

The next morning, I mustered up enough energy to cook breakfast for Tristan and I since Demetri stayed at his own place last night. I had to act as if my stomach wasn't doing flips while I was at work. I had forgotten how pregnancy can wreck pure havoc on a woman's body. Men were so lucky. I was relieved that today would be an early work day for me since Tristan had an important basketball game tonight. They were playing against Vincent High School whose team was also decorated with talented players. With these two powerhouse teams going against each other in their conference, it had been declared as Game of the Week and would be televised. I left work early after my last appointment and headed home to get ready for the game. I didn't really feel like dressing up, but I didn't want my appearance to match my mood so I concluded that a hoodie and yoga pants were out of the question. I had a few hours to spare so I decided to pamper myself in hopes of feeling better.

I went to the nail shop for a manicure and pedicure before heading to the hair salon to get my hair straighten. I preferred the curly look over the straight style, but I did it every now and then to switch it up see the true length of my hair since shrinkage is real for curly girls. I felt a little better after my spa day but my stomach still felt as if it was doing back flips. Oh well, at least I looked good on the outside though. I was dressed and waiting for Demetri to come pick me up so we could go to the game. I was glad that the coach decided not to suspend Tristan from playing after his fight the other day. He knew that if they had a good chance of winning Tristan needed to be on the floor.

Demetri finally arrived and he was on time as always. He was looking as if he'd stepped out of a GQ magazine. He always dressed to impress but his attire tonight was more than casual for a basketball game. He had a fresh haircut and was exuding sex appeal with ease. If we didn't have Tristan's game to attend, I would have put it on him right then and there. I don't know if it was my pregnancy hormones but my sex drive had been through the roof lately. Did I mention that he was looking edible as hell? Damn!

"Look at you looking like you belong in the GQ magazine." He definitely earned that compliment and then some.

"No, look at you with your hair straight! I've never seen it straight before. It looks good. You ready to leave?"

"Yeah, just let me set the alarm and lock up."

After I locked and secured my house we walked hand in hand to his truck. He kept staring at me and smiling the entire time we drove to Tristan's school. He told me that he and Tristan were actually on good terms and he now supported our relationship. This was such a relief for me because I care about my son's happiness and the fact that he's embracing another man being in the picture suggests that he's finally dealing with his father's death in a healthy manner. This made me enthusiastic about the future endeavors of our family.

Due to this game being televised, it was packed more than usual. I was glad that we arrived early so we could still get a decent seat despite the crowd. The teams were warming up when I noticed Tristan and made eye contact with him. It had been years since I'd seen him this happy. My hormones were working overtime already with the pregnancy so this almost made me shed tears of joy. I could see the kid that Tristan had fought sitting on the bench with a black eye. I couldn't help but feel sorry for him because I could only imagine how bad Tristan must have lashed out on him. I'm not a fan of violence unless it's absolutely necessary. The game was finally starting. Vincent won the jump ball and immediately scored. I could tell that this was going to be a close game, but I had faith in my son and his team because athleticism was something that just came naturally for him. There was about five seconds left in the second quarter when a player from Vincent landed a three point shot at the buzzer and tied the score. The band usually performed during halftime, but they weren't on the floor to play. Instead, Tristan was in the middle of the floor with a microphone in his hands for something he claimed was a special ceremony. I didn't know anything about this so I was anxious to find out what was going on.

"I would like to take this time to formally tell my number one supporter, my mother how much I love and appreciate her for shaping me into the man I am today and keeping me on a path to success. Do me a favor and come stand next to me, Ma." Tristan motioned his hand for me to come down on the court.

I didn't know what this was about but I did as I was asked and made my way to the middle of the gymnasium where Tristan stood. Demetri had gone to the bathroom a little while before halftime and then to the concession stand to grab us some snacks. I was nervous because all eyes were on me and I still had no idea exactly what was going on. Tristan placed his arm over my shoulder when I stood next to him and continued his speech. Suddenly, I heard my favorite song "You" by Jesse Powell playing in the background as he continued talking.

"You've sacrificed so much to allow me to be in the place where I am now, and even sacrificed your own happiness at times. I want to take this time to say thank you and to let everyone watching know that if anyone deserves to be happy it's definitely you, Ma. I have a surprise for you but I need you to close your eyes for me."

I closed my eyes and now my nerves were all over the place wondering what was going to happen next. I was still hearing my favorite song in the background and a few moments had passed when Tristan informed me that I can now open my eyes, and when I did, I was shocked beyond belief. Demetri was down on one knee with a jewelry box in his hands while Tristan held the microphone to his mouth. I couldn't believe what was happening before my eyes.

"Kelsey, I've been waiting on this moment since the day I met you. I've never met a woman that's genuinely beautiful inside and out. I hope that you'll give me the honors of taking my last name because I want to be yours only from this day forth. I want to spend the rest of my life making you smile and laugh. Baby I love you with all of my heart. Will you marry me?"

The water works were running down my cheeks now. I screamed yes in between sobs and kissed him as he picked me up and embraced me while the people in the crowd cheered us on. I was beyond happy and at a loss for words. I decided I was going to tell him that we were expecting a bundle of joy after the game. The Most High definitely works in mysterious ways. I noticed that Demetri's parents were in in the stands when we made it back to our seats, and behind them sat Marcus and Kendra. Everyone was in on the secret except for me! This was a moment in my life that I would never forget. Mrs. Latimore was the first to approach me after the proposal. She hugged me and kissed my cheek.

"Congratulations! I don't think you understand how happy we are to have you as our daughter-in-law! It's about time you two stopped playing games. If you need help planning the wedding, you know that

I am more than willing to help right?" she asked with both hands resting on my shoulders.

"You already know that you will be the first person I call Mrs. Latimore", I smiled at her.

"Mrs. Latimore is how strangers address me. You can call me mama from now on, and might I add that you are glowing by the way", she smiled a knowingly smirk.

"Thank you and I appreciate the warm welcome mama."

"No need to thank me Kelsey. The pleasure is all mines."

Mr. Latimore, Marcus, and Kendra finally joined the huddle and congratulated us as well. We all continued chatting until the game resumed. I couldn't help but stare at the huge rock that now decorated my finger. It had been a few years since I'd worn a wedding ring, but this one was drop dead gorgeous. Demetri had really outdone himself. Tristan's team ended up winning by one point which made the game quite entertaining to watch. He decided to stay over his teammates house for the weekend to give us some alone time I'm assuming. I couldn't stop smiling on our way home and it was taking everything in me to not tell Demetri about the pregnancy just yet. I think his mother knows about my pregnancy somehow, but I didn't want to probe her in front of Demetri. I was waiting for the perfect moment to tell him the news. When we made it back to my place he and I posted in the kitchen. I sat on top of the kitchen counter as he poured us some red wine to celebrate the proposal. I felt as if this was the perfect time to inform him.

"Baby, I have something to tell you." I don't know why I was so nervous.

"Is it good or bad?" he questioned as he handed me a glass of wine.

"I would hope that it's good news."

"I'll be the judge of that. What is it?" he asked as he sipped his drink.

"I'm pregnant. Two weeks pregnant to be exact."

"Seriously?" he was smiling harder than ever.

"Yeah, I found out this morning."

"You know what this means right?"

"What?"

"We should get married before the baby comes, if that's cool with you?" he stated with confidence as if this had been his plan all along.

"That's funny because I was thinking the same thing", I chuckled. We seemed to have a way of thinking the same thing at times.

"Great minds think alike. So how do you want to go about it?"

"That depends on if you want to have a wedding or go to the courthouse."

"Well, I want to experience a wedding with you. I want to see you walking down the aisle in a beautiful white dress."

"I guess if we're going to have a wedding, we better start planning soon."

"Yeah, I'll see if Derek's wife will help out with the planning. I hope you know that I might be smothering you now that I know that you're carrying my seed and for the next nine months I'm not pulling out." he chuckled and nestled in between my legs.

"You are so silly" I kissed those sexy lips of his and wrapped my arms around his neck.

I was still sitting on of the kitchen counter with him nestled in between my thighs as he gently kissed my neck. Our kisses led to him stripping down to his briefs and me shirtless. He picked me up from the counter, carried me to the bedroom and laid me on the bed. He pulled my panties down and buried his face in between my thighs. My hormones from the pregnancy must have heightened my senses because the sensations he was giving me from sucking my clit and rubbing my breast seemed more amplified than before.

"Oh my God, Demetri," was all I could scream as I trembled from an earthshaking orgasm. He finally came up for air and kissed my lips. I loved the way he puts my body on a pedestal and made sure to never neglect one inch of me. I pushed him back on the bed and got on top of him. I started kissing on a spot that I knew made him weak for me. I felt his dick get as hard as it get could under me. It was definitely begging for some attention. I kissed my way down his chest and licked his nipples along the way. I licked a trail down to his dick and engulfed a mouth full of him. Normally, I would tease him with sucking on the tip but I was in a freaky mood tonight. I gave him what he was yearning for and I knew how to do it well if I must say so myself. As always I enjoyed the moans coming from him. I stopped giving him head and immediately eased down on his dick because I couldn't wait any longer. He instantly started gripping my hips and ass as I rode him like a porn star. I was going up and down like a rollercoaster as his hands aimlessly roamed all over my body. He was making so many different sexy faces and it turned me on to no end.

"Fuck, I'm about to come", he moaned. I wasn't ready for this ride to end just yet.

"Don't come yet baby, I'm almost there." I didn't want him to come yet so I crawled off of him and waited on my hands and knees with my back arched and ass in the air for his taking. He got the point and slid in from the back. This was starting to become my favorite position. It was something about this position that just brought out the hood in a man. Demetri was nowhere near hood but you couldn't tell when he was hitting it from the back. I wanted him to pull my hair and then some. I was going crazy when he found that magical spot.

“Pull my hair," I moaned to him in between the smacking noises. He grabbed a handful of hair and pulled it as requested. I was gripping and pulling the covers and biting my lower lip to keep from disturbing the neighborhood. I was about to come and I could tell that Demetri couldn't hold his nut any longer. I was throwing it back in sync with his thrusts and looking back at him to see how he was handling it. I couldn't help but dig my nails into the pillow and burry my face to smother my screams. I moaned and called him daddy when he pulled my hair again as my juices came down onto him.

Demetri kept his promise and didn't pull out when he came. I felt him throbbing and jerking from the aftermath of busting a nut and at the moment I felt like no one else could compete against us when we're in the sheets.

We lay naked in bed wrapped around each other as we caught our breaths from our sex session. I was still horny after round one and I was hoping that Demetri could get up for round two. I crawled on top of him and straddled his waist. My plan was to get him back hard which shouldn't have been too difficult since I knew his body so well and all his spots to turn him on. I kissed the side of his neck and twirled my tongue in the circular motion the way he loves before biting down on his ear lobe. I made sure to sway my breast in his face because I know he loved how they sat up. I felt him growing hard again and I eased my way down his body to give him head again. His hands cupped the back of my head encouraging me to go as deep as I could. I never had a problem deep throating him and this occasion wouldn't be any different. After giving him head, I took him by the hand and led him to the bathroom. I turned the shower on and pulled him in to get wet with me. I kneeled back down and deep throated him again as the water cascaded down my back. He cupped the back of my head again and moaned. I wanted some back shots again so I turned around and arched my back just the way that he liked. He slid the tip in, gripped my hips and stroked at a slow pace. We both moaned in unison and enjoyed the sensations we were giving one another. He was grinding slow and taking his time which was fine with me because it was passionate and I was enjoying every inch of him. I dug my nails in the back of his thighs as he moaned. I was scratching his legs up because I was on the verge of coming so hard and I could tell her sensed it too. He pulled my hair and continued slow stroking me and hitting my spot every time. I shuddered and came all over his dick and this time I didn't try to mute my screams. Demetri came and moaned something serious. Again he didn't pull out and I felt him throbbing inside me. After the amazing sex we had my hair was no longer straight. It had reverted back to its curly state. We were back in bed cuddling after we showered and not really watching the movie we had put in because we were too busy discussing our new bundle of joy and our plans for the future. We decided that we would start looking for a house together to accommodate our growing family. To say the least, I was excited for our new beginnings.

Chapter Ten:

Karma

Now ain't this a bitch? I couldn't believe my eyes as I sat in the bar watching this so called basketball game of the week. I wasn't nearly interested in it until I happened to glance at the screen and noticed Demetri proposing to my former psychologist. I called over the bartender and ordered some more shots to help me forget about the shitty day I was already having and this proposal was just the icing on the cake. I was fired from my law firm which happened to be Demetri's and his father's firm. How stupid could I have been? How come I didn't see this bitch plotting on me when I met her? She took my man, my apartment and now my job! I definitely underestimated Dr. Smith. I bet she and Demetri enjoyed a hearty laugh at my expense. She probably went back and informed him of all of the wrongdoings that I told her in confidence and used it against me to steal my man. I was so angry that I felt as if fire was running through my veins. The happiness that oozed from them through the flat screen pissed me off even more. The next thing I knew Sassy was in my head telling me that this bitch needed to be handled so that I could reclaim what was rightfully mine. I had nothing but time on my hands since I was fired from the firm and blackballed from being hired at other firms thanks to Mr. Latimore. First thing in the morning, I'll be tracking Demetri's every move to see where his new bitch lives. I told him that I wasn't going anywhere and I meant it.

The next morning I woke up on a mission. I was now staying in a rundown, one bedroom apartment since I was running low on the life insurance money I inherited from my parents' deaths. I loved living lavishly but now the bills were starting to catch up with me. I was more financially stable when I was with Demetri because he gave me whatever I wanted until he cut me off to be with that bitch. I switched cars with a friend so that I wouldn't be detected by him while I trailed his every move. I disguised myself with a blond wig, a hat and sunglasses. I already knew his daily routine like the back of my hand because it was so predictable. His life consisted of working at the firm, going to the gym, church, and visiting his family. He should be up getting ready for work right about now if my assumptions were correct. I assumed he was staying at his apartment so I planned on taking a trip to his place, but if he was at his bitch's house then I'd wait for him at the firm. I was pissed when I made it to his apartment complex because his car was nowhere in sight which meant he was probably lying up with that trick. I pulled off and made my way to the law firm downtown. I made it there a few minutes before the time he usually reports to work. I parked in a low-key part of the lot, shut the car off and patiently waited for Demetri to arrive. I was messing around with my phone when I noticed Demetri pull up in his Range Rover. The Buick must have still been in the shop getting repaired. He stepped out of his truck looking fine as hell in a fitted black button up and black slacks. He was smiling from ear to ear and seeing him so giddy knowing that I was not the reason for his smiles fueled my anger. I noticed that he went and got more tailored suits too after I destroyed all of his old ones. He went inside the building without detecting me. I waited in the car as if I was a cop on a stakeout with my snacks and phone handy. I knew he took his lunch break around noon and he usually leaves for lunch so if he did today, I'd follow him.

It was around 12:15 P.M. when Demetri exited the building with a smile still sketched across his face. He hopped inside his truck without realizing I was following him like his shadow. He stopped at a restaurant and grabbed some food before making his way to Dr. Smith's office. I knew because I took this same route to her office for my therapy session with her. I was beyond pissed and it took every ounce in me to remain calm so I wouldn't blow my cover. He couldn't park his car fast enough when he pulled into the lot. He quickly hopped out of his truck and loosened the tie he was wearing as he made his way to the front of the building. I waited in the parking lot of a business that was adjacent to Dr. Smith's office so that I could see everything without being noticed. He stayed inside the building for over an hour and a half. His lunch breaks were never that long when I was working at the firm. I studied his behavior as he exited the double doors to her office and I could tell that he just had sex. He was buttoning up the shirt he had on and was smiling like the joker as he practically skipped his way to his truck. I was so angry that smoke was probably steaming from my ears. How dare he disrespect me like that for this bitch? I was on his coattail when he left her office and went back to his law firm for the remainder of the day. I followed him once he left work around 4:30 in the afternoon. He was cruising down I-43 South and headed to a place I'd never been before. He made a right onto a block in a Mequon neighborhood that screamed, "I got money for days!" He pulled into a driveway that was decorated with a beautiful green manicured lawn and an all brick mini-mansion that was outlined with an olive color. It was beautiful to say the least. He shut his car off, knocked on the front door and waited for someone to answer. When I saw who opened the door for him, I had fire running through my veins again. Demetri bent down, kissed and rubbed her belly, and then stood to kiss her lips. I know this trick not pregnant with his baby! She knows I can't have kids and she used that against me to take my man! She has another thing coming if she thinks I'll let her play house and have a happily ever after with Demetri. After I stopped trailing him I went back to my place to get my game plan in motion. Her belly didn't look like she was months pregnant which meant I had some time to get my shit in order.

I was staring at my reflection with both hands planted firmly on a dingy sink that had a permanent dirt stain around the rim of it. How could Demetri window shop for other women when he owns this right here? What man in his right mind wouldn't treasure the ground I walked on? I mean, just look at me. My body was on point and let's not forget to mention that I was as smart as they come. I was literally the epitome of beauty and brains so why did he leave me for that bitch? My anger was rising inside of me and I felt the need to calm down so I took a few deep breaths to relax but it wasn't working. I opened the foggy mirror of the medicine cabinet and grabbed the bottle of pills that I was supposed to be taking on a daily basis. It doped me up every time and I was only a shell of myself whenever I took them, which was why I hadn't taken them in a while. I was about to pop one in my mouth when Sassy appeared and smacked them out of my hands.

"What the hell do you think you're doing? If you take that shit you know I can't come around right? Is that what you want? Who's going to protect you if I'm not around?"

"But I..."

"But nothing! I told you what happens if you take that shit! Now give me that bottle!" Sassy quickly snatched the bottle of pills and flushed them down the toilet along with my other medications for my schizophrenic and bipolar disorder. Ever since I was little girl she took control and handled anything that I couldn't. She'd always been by my side no matter what.

"Now you listen to me, the last thing we need right now is for you to be doped up during a time like this. That bitch plotted against you and took your man and you're telling me the answer to that is to take your medication? No! The answer is to get revenge and take back what's yours by any means necessary and I have just the thing in mind for little miss Dr. Smith! So are you down with this or do I have to recruit others for the plan?"

"You know if you're down, I'm down with you. So what's the plan Sassy?" I asked as I studied her facial expression the mirror.

"Don't worry about it right now. I'll tell you when the time is right because I don't want you getting cold feet. Okay?"

"Yeah, I hear you."

Sassy went back to her special place and I was left alone to ponder my thoughts. I was racking my brain trying to come up with a plan to handle Dr. Smith and this baby. Should I kidnap her and kill her before the baby comes? Should I wait until after she has the baby and kill the baby? There were just so many different options that I didn't know what to choose. I decided to sleep on it and make a decision in the morning. It was back to trailing Demetri tomorrow to gather as much information as I could about him and his bitch.

The next morning I woke up and continued the same routine of following Demetri and gathering intelligence on his every move. Seeing how much he loved and treasured Dr. Smith mad my blood boil so much so that I almost intentionally rear-ended him out of spite. I decided to wait until they least expected it and put my plan in motion when the baby comes. They'd have their guard down and I'd probably be a distant memory to them by then. Little Miss Dr. Smith just didn't know what type of storm was heading her way.

Part Two

Chapter Eleven:

Demetri

She's so beautiful! I was holding my baby girl for the first time since Kelsey had pushed her out. She was born at 1:23 A.M. on November 24th weighing five pounds, eight ounces and measuring at 23 inches long. This was the happiest day of my life and it was destiny that I had a child with the woman I'd always wanted so that's what we decided to name her. Her name was Destiny Ryan Latimore and she had beautiful hazel eyes just like me. Kelsey and I decided to have an at home birth in our new home with a midwife. We wanted an intimate setting and more control of the labor and formalities of our baby girl regarding vaccinations. She had a natural birth and I thanked her every minute on the minute for enduring labor pains without any type of epidural. We had a wonderful nine months together before bringing our blessing into this world. I enjoyed my daughter's kicks and I spoke to Kelsey's stomach every chance I got. I wouldn't let Kelsey lift a finger while she was pregnant. I did all of the cooking and household chores with the help of Tristan of course. This was an experience that I wanted to relive with Kelsey over and over again and if it was up to me, she would stay barefoot and pregnant, but I know she loved her patients too much to give that up.

We had an elegant yet simple wedding thanks to my mom and Derek's wife, Lisa. We decided to have the wedding two months after we found out we were expecting because Kelsey said she didn't want to feel like a whale on our wedding. I still remember that feeling in the pit of my stomach when I seen her walking down the aisle. It was the same feeling I had when I first met her on freshman move-in day of college, only then she was wearing a gray sundress that accentuated her curves. She looked so angelic back then and the gracefulness of her natural state never changed. My parents were more than happy when we told them we were expecting a baby. My mother couldn't hold her composure and informed us that she already seen the pregnancy glow on Kelsey at the game. I felt like the luckiest man on earth with everything falling into place so perfectly. Tristan was more than happy about having a baby sister even though he was now attending college in Kentucky. He kept in touch with us every day and visited a couple times a month, and yes he was still holding onto his virginity despite all the temptation. I was proud of him.

The midwife made sure that Kelsey's placenta had been fully pushed out with the baby by pushing down on her stomach. She grimaced as if she was in pain so I tried my best to console her by rubbing her arm. I hated seeing her in pain. After the midwife washed Destiny's hair and gave her a bath, she left us alone to enjoy our new bundle of joy. Kelsey was exhausted but the midwife told us to try to get Destiny to latch onto her breast so that she could get used to breastfeeding. I picked her up and brought her close to Kelsey so that she could breastfeed. It was like second nature to Destiny and she latched on immediately. I couldn't stop smiling as I watched my two favorite girls bond for the first time. I pulled my phone out and took pictures because this was a moment I always wanted to cherish. After Kelsey was done breastfeeding, I took Destiny to let her relax while I bonded with our baby. I placed her on my chest with my shirt off since the midwife told me that newborn babies love skin to skin contact. Surprisingly, this was so soothing and relaxing. I could tell she wasn't going to be one of those babies who cried around the clock. I picked up her little pinky and twirled my finger around hers. I see a smile creep on her face and my heart melted. She was definitely going to be daddy's little princess. I glanced over at Kelsey and noticed that she was knocked out. She still looked beautiful even with her hair in disarray.

I pulled out my phone and sent pictures to my parents, Marcus and Kendra. My mother was a little upset that we decided not to have any visitors during the birth and a few days after the birth because we wanted to enjoy these precious moments as a family, but she understood where we were coming from so she didn't have any hard feelings. Tristan would be visiting in a few days to meet his baby sister and see the new house since he hadn't seen it since we moved in. We figured he'd want his own space whenever he came home so we had a guest house built behind our house just for him. We decided to surprise him with the guest house as a way of letting him know just how much we were proud of him and all of his accomplishments. Marcus broke down and finally admitted that he was indeed in love with Kendra. He proposed to her on their one year anniversary and of course I had to give him tips on how to go about it, but everything went smoothly. After watching Kelsey and I go through our pregnancy, he had baby fever. The first question he asked when I told him Kelsey was pregnant was, "Is it true what they say about pregnant pussy?" Sex is literally what Marcus thinks about 90% of the time. “Of course," I told him. It was definitely true and ever since then he'd been talking about having babies. I know he's something else but he's still my homie.

I decided to let Kelsey rest while I spent some daddy-daughter time with my princess. She had a head full of curly hair and she really resembled me more than she did Kelsey. I went to her nursery and sat in the rocking chair with her cradled to my chest. She still had yet to cry since she'd been in this world and she seemed so relaxed in my embrace. She looked so angelic as she slept and held my pinky close to her chest. After she fell asleep, I put her on her back in her crib and watched her for a while. I definitely wanted more kids. At least another boy and a girl and then I'd be satisfied. I turned on the baby monitors and left one in her nursery. I went back to our makeshift hospital room and crawled in bed next to Kelsey as she slept peacefully. I was grateful for this woman next to me and I didn't mind showing it. She knew how much I loved and appreciated her every day. I cuddled close to her and placed my arm around her waist. I didn't want to wake her so I didn't pull her as close as we usually slept. I also didn't want to cause her anymore pain. I finally dozed off around three in the morning until I felt Kelsey moving from under me.

"Baby what's wrong?" I was still tired and rubbing my eyes. My words were muffled as my face was still buried in the pillow.

"I had a nightmare. Something isn't right Demetri. Go check on Destiny for me.", she claimed as she sat up in the bed.

"She's fine babe. I just put her to sleep and I have the baby monitor right here with me. She's fine", I stated sternly because she knew how I felt about my sleep. I could get rather moody when I'm lacking it.

"Babe can you just do it? I'll feel a lot better and I'll let you go back to sleep. It'll give me a peace of mind", she pleaded.

"Alright. I'll be right back." I crawled out of bed and went down the hall to check on Destiny. She was still silently sleeping in her crib just the way I left her. I returned back to our guest room/makeshift hospital room.

"She's fine. She's still sleeping in the same spot I left her in. Just get some rest for now."

"Did you check to see if she was breathing?"

"Yes, Kelsey. She's breathing just fine. Can I get some sleep now?" I wasn't irritated with her. I just get cranky sometimes when I'm exhausted.

"Okay, I'm sorry. Go back to sleep. I'll just listen to the baby monitor for a while."

"Try to get some sleep. I think you need it more than I do."

"After the nightmare I just had, I can't go back to sleep right now. You can go to sleep. I'll be up for a while."

"You just said the magic words. I'm exhausted anyway, but wake me up if you need me." I kissed her on the lips and rolled over onto my right side.

For the next two days, Kelsey and I bonded with our daughter. It was a beautiful experience despite the fact that Kelsey was growing more and more paranoid about Destiny's safety. I'm assuming she may be going through some hormonal changes from post-pregnancy and possibly postpartum depression. She'd been having nightmares since she gave birth and she was convinced that something was wrong but she couldn't elaborate on why she felt this way; she claimed it was her intuition telling her that something was off. I didn't know how to handle this and I was happy that my parents were coming to visit us today. I was hoping that my mother could shed some light on what was going on with Kelsey because I was feeling helpless. I watched through the window and seen my dad pull into the driveway. I met them at the car to tell them what was going on with Kelsey because I didn't want her to think that I thought she was going crazy. My mother immediately understood where I was coming from.

"Demetri give her body some time to adjust back into the swing of things. She just had a baby and sometimes a woman's hormones can still be all over of the place. Things will get back to normal soon", she assured me.

"I don't know about that, Ma. I've never seen her so paranoid in my life. She's talking about getting a tracking device so we can make sure Destiny is safe. Is that normal to you?"

"After having a baby, yes I'd say it's normal. That's just something that you'll never understand. Now where's my little princess?"

I opened the front door and led them upstairs to the nursery where Kelsey was breastfeeding Destiny. My mother was smiling from ear to ear as she looked down at Destiny and it put a smile on my face too. I grabbed a blanket to cover up Kelsey since my dad was in the room. After she finished feeding Destiny, my mother washed her hands and immediately took my princess from my arms. She gently kissed her granddaughter and had baby talk. My dad and I decided to give the girls some time to bond as we went down to my man cave in the basement.

"So how are you enjoying fatherhood so far?" pops asked as he picked up the pool stick.

"I love it! I can't imagine life without Destiny being in it and she's only been here a few days. Plus, she barely even cries which is surprising. She's definitely going to be my spoiled little princess", I stated as I set the balls up to start a game of pool.

"Yeah, and it only gets better from here. Just wait until she starts talking. That's when things get interesting."

"I can wait until then. Right now, I just want to enjoy her infancy. So how's business since I've been away?" I asked as I took the first shot to break, sinking one stripped ball.

"Business is afloat as usual, but I've been hearing through the grapevine that your ex-fiancée isn't doing too well financially. You know I have eyes and ears everywhere", pops claimed as he searched for the best angle to hit a solid ball in the pocket.

"Maybe if she knew how to control her anger she wouldn't be struggling. What did you hear about her?"

"Well, last I heard, she finally got a gig being a paralegal for some small firm downtown, but she's not bringing in nearly as much as she was making with us. I heard she's on the verge of having that treasured Mercedes repossessed."

"I hate to say this but I don't feel sorry for her. I do wish her the best though." It was now my turn since pops missed.

"She's a smart girl. I'm sure she'll get it together eventually."

"Yeah, she's definitely smart, and don't forget crazy. Enough about her though. How did Ma react after she gave birth to me?"

"Your mother was experiencing mood swings after she gave birth to you but it went away once you were a few weeks old. Just be patient with Kelsey, her body is going through a lot of changes that us men will never fathom."

"This seems a lot different from mood swings though. It seems like something more serious than that", I stated as I laid the pool stick down on the table to focus more on the conversation rather than the game.

"Just keep an eye on her and pray for the best."

"Yeah, I hear you Pops."

We went back upstairs to check on the girls and see how everyone was doing. Destiny was sleeping in her crib while my mama and Kelsey were chatting. It seemed as if they were having an important conversation so I didn't intervene. My dad had some errands to run so I walked my parents to the truck to wish them goodbye.

"Demetri, I don't think Kelsey is exaggerating. I don't want to scare you, but a mother knows when their child is in danger. Just listen to her with an open mind and don't judge her, okay?"

"Ma, what did she say to you?" I asked as I opened the passenger door.

"Just listen to your wife, she's not crazy. I'll see you guys soon. Love you."

She embraced me and gave me a hug. My dad did his usual dap handshake before pulling off. Now I was worried sick wondering if Destiny was truly in danger or not. I still believed it was the hormones talking, so that's what I chalked it up too. I spent the rest of the day relaxing with Destiny on my chest. Kelsey said she wanted to run to the mall to get some fresh air and buy some things for Destiny so it was just me and my baby girl for a few hours. When Kelsey returned, she had bags full of clothes as if Destiny didn't have a room full of clothes already. She also bought her a beautiful gold bracelet with her name ingrained on it. It just so happened to fit her wrist perfectly. We chilled in our bedroom and watched movies for the rest of the day with Destiny laying on the bed in between us. This was all I needed.

The next day Kendra and Marcus paid us a visit and fell in love with Destiny. They were excited about jumping the broom and soon starting a family of their own. Marcus always claimed that he wanted to have only boys, but when he picked up Destiny for the first time, he quickly changed his mind. They stayed with us the entire day and Kendra really didn't want to leave. She told me that she would babysit anytime. Just give her a call. After Kelsey breastfed Destiny, I bathed and put her to sleep in her nursery before running a bubble bath for Kelsey since she was still healing from labor and needed to relax. I lit some candles, turned off the lights and put on one of her favorite slow jams playlist. I poured her a glass of red wine since the doctor said it was okay to drink wine while she breastfed. I woke her up and led her to the bathroom. She smiled when she noticed my gesture of romance. We hadn't had sex since she gave birth but she pleased me in other ways. I wasn't really worried about sex anyway, I just wanted her to heal properly. She slipped out of the t-shirt and jogging pants she was wearing and put her hair into a bun.

She eased down into the water and immediately exhaled. She was still attractive to me even with the pregnancy weight she had gained. She was already talking about hitting the gym with Kendra once she fully healed. I made sure to tell her that she still looked beautiful even after pregnancy. I know she'll never admit it but I knew the weight gain made her feel somewhat insecure so I was always complimented her because I wanted her to know that I had no intentions of going anywhere. I picked up her loofah and washed her back and neck for her. I knew that she can clean herself, I just wanted to show her my appreciation for giving me the greatest gift known to man. I figured it was the least I could do after she endured pregnancy and labor. She smiled at me.

“I really do appreciate you doing this Demetri. I know I may be unpleasant to be around lately but I do love you for understanding”, she said as she let out a sigh.

“It’s cool babe, I don't know what pregnancy is like so all I can do is try to understand. How are you feeling?”

“I feel more relaxed now thanks to you. I just hope I can stay that way when I go to sleep.” I tensed up at the thought of her having another nightmare, which meant another sleepless night for me.

"Let's just hope the nightmares will stop soon. Maybe it's just a postpartum thing", I hoped.

"Yeah, hopefully. You know you can join me anytime right? We have some time before Destiny wakes up and I want to show you how much I appreciate you", she said seductively. I already knew what that meant.

"You ain't said nothing but a word."

I stripped out of my jogging pants and T-shirt and was about to fully undress until I thought I heard Destiny crying so I went to her room to check on her. She was still sleeping so I went back to join Kelsey in the bath. I already knew what she meant when she said she wanted to show her appreciation and I was down with getting head from her any day. I was sitting on the edge of the tub when she crawled between my legs and put the tip of my dick in her mouth. I moaned at the instant warmth of her mouth and tongue. She eased her way down my shaft and deep throated my dick. I gripped the back of her head and moaned. It was something about the way she sucked my dick like she was making love to it. The way she had my head spinning, I already knew I was gone come faster than the police in white neighborhoods. I was at a point where I couldn't hold my nut back any longer. She deep throated me one last time before I gripped the back of her head and came in her mouth. I held her in that position until my body stopped jerking. I never did that to her before but she didn't protest when she let go of my dick. She just smiled at me because she knew she had me wrapped around her fingers. My body was tingling and riddled with aftershock. She had me stuck.

“Fuck,” was the only thing I could muster.

“I love you.” She kissed me then grabbed a towel to dry off.

“I love you too.”

I smacked her on her ass as she stepped out of the tub still dripping wet. She had gained weight in all the right places if you were to ask me. I checked on Destiny again before I retreated to our bedroom and crawled under the sheets with Kelsey; she was already fast asleep. Destiny barely woke up throughout the night. I think she was the only baby I’d ever known who barely cried and didn’t constantly wake up throughout the middle of the night. I hope she keeps this up because I haven't had much sleep lately due to Kelsey's nightmares. Thank God Pops was picking up my slack while I was on paternity leave because I would be dead tired if I still had to get up and go to work. I was in a deep slumber until I felt Kelsey jumping and talking in her sleep. I sat up and watched her to see what was going on with her. She scared the shit out of me when she started screaming and yelling so I woke her up.

"You okay?" I couldn't mask my concern any longer. I was really starting to worry now.

"Yeah, I'm good babe. Just go back to sleep", she sated nonchalantly as if it was nothing.

"You do realize that you were just screaming at the top of your lungs right? You expect me to go back to sleep after that?"

"Can you just hold me until I fall back to sleep?" Her expression told me that she didn't want to discuss this topic anymore so I didn't probe her any further.

"Come here", I demanded.

I scooted closer to her and wrapped my arms around her. I was starting to stress about her mental state now. I know my mother said this phase would pass, but I couldn't help but worry about this. She was still paranoid about Destiny even though she was a couple of weeks old now. I did a silent prayer while she was wrapped in my arms. I prayed for Kelsey to bounce back from her postpartum depression.

Chapter Twelve:

Marcus

It was getting close to the time for us to start planning our wedding and I was shocked to be so excited about getting married. I finally introduced Kendra to my Uncle Sir and he loved her. He said she was perfect for me. If she could pass his test then she was definitely a keeper. We still had our own apartments but we had already started looking for a home to buy. I couldn't believe just how much I had changed within two years but I guess meeting that one special person would do that to a man like me. The first thing I planned on doing once we were married was to get her pregnant. Seeing Demetri with his daughter made me want a daughter just as much as I needed my next breath.

I had just finished working out and I was on my way home to shower and change clothes. For some reason, Tasha had been calling and texting me like crazy so I eventually changed my number when she didn't get the hint that I was done with her ass for good. What happened to "lose my number?" Ever since that day, she had been blowing up my phone. I was convinced that some women were just psychotic. I was so glad that wasn't the case with my baby Kendra. She'd always been the laid-back, stress-free type of female that I loved. I pulled into my driveway and hopped out of the car. I left the front door unlocked for Kendra since she had lost her house keys again and I hadn't made the time to get another set. She should've been on her way to my place by now and I didn't want to hop out of the shower to open the door for her.

I stripped out of my clothes, turned the water on and waited for it to heat up. I brushed my waves before hopping in the shower and of course I used my favorite shower gel from Bath and Body Works. I was obsessed with their *Whitewater Rush* scent. I thought I heard movement in the house so I assumed Kendra had finally made it home. I stepped out the shower, wiped the fog from my mirror and wrapped a towel around my waist. I left the bathroom and was about to go to my bedroom to put some clothes on when I heard more movement coming from my living room. My jaw dropped when I see who was sitting on my sofa as if she belonged here.

"What the fuck is you doing in my house Tasha and how the fuck do you know where I live?" I was pissed and paranoid because I knew Kendra was due here any minute and I could see all hell breaking loose if she walked in the door and seen this trick sitting here.

“Don't act like you not happy to see me Marcus. I know you’ve missed me as much as I’ve missed you.”

“The only thing I’ve missed is not having to put up with your bipolar ass. Now get out of my house, right now!”

I was trying to push her out the front door without being too rough with her ass but she was pushing back and refusing to leave. She was all over me. She tried to kiss on my neck and my chest while I continued to push her away from me. She had pulled my towel a loose and it fell to the floor leaving me completely naked and exposed. I was about to pick it up, wrap it back around my waist and kick her ass out when Kendra opened the door with bags of food in her hands. Tasha had her arms wrapped around my waist trying to claim what she thought was hers. The look on her face broke my heart when she caught me standing in the living room butt-ass naked with Tasha all over me. I knew what it looked like and I knew she wasn’t going to believe me when I was going to tell her that I did nothing wrong. I could see the pain in her eyes and anger boiling inside of her. Tasha's dumb ass was smirking and still standing there as if her life wasn't in jeopardy. Now I was confident that this bitch was crazy and I should have never fucked with her in the first place. Kendra dropped the bags of food and stormed out of my house. I totally forgot that I was butt-ass naked when I pushed Tasha off of me and chased after Kendra to plead my case. I didn't give a damn about my nakedness because I was a desperate man who was about to lose the only woman I'd ever loved.

"Baby wait! I swear it's not what it looks like. Just give me a minute to explain what happened!" I yelled after her as she rushed out the door.

"Don't baby me, Marcus! How can you explain you being butt-ass naked with that bitch all over you in your house? How could you do this to me of all people?" she yelled at the top of her lungs.

"Baby, I swear I didn't fuck her! You have to believe me when I say I didn't touch her and I would never disrespect you like that! Baby, please just listen to me…"

I tried to grab her by the arm and pull her close to me but she pulled back, cocked her arm back as far as it could go and punched me in my right eye. I'm not going to lie. That shit had me dazed for a second. I didn't know she could pack a punch like that. She hopped in her car and pulled off leaving me there dazed and naked on the side of the curb. I couldn't believe what just happened. I was still sitting on the curb butt-ass naked, deep in my thoughts when a family came out of the building and cursed me out for exposing myself to their kids. I ran back in the house and lost it because this bitch had the nerve to still be in my crib as if she didn't just ruin my fucking life. I had to really calm down because if I didn't, I was surely going to jail for assault and battery. Better yet, possibly murder if she didn't get the fuck out of my house. She was back sitting on the sofa with her legs crossed just as calm and collected as I was trying to be. I grabbed my towel off of the floor and wrapped myself up. She didn't deserve to see me naked.

"Tasha I'm only going to say this one time, and I do mean ONE time… get the fuck out of my crib before I seriously put my hands on you! Trust me when I say I will get away with it too! Don't forget that I know people who know people! Now, I'm going to ask you this. 'Do you want to walk out of here or do you want to crawl out of here beaten and bruised?'" She stood and just stared at me.

"I've been watching you for a while now and I can tell that you really love her as much as I loved you. This is your karma for being such an asshole to women Marcus! I did what I came here to do anyway. Goodbye, Marcus."

"Crazy bitch," I yelled to her as she slammed the door behind her. I grabbed my phone and immediately called Kendra but her phone kept going straight to voicemail. I lost count of how many voicemails and text messages I left her that day. I broke down and cried for the first time ever over a woman. Now I could understand what a broken heart truly felt like. I felt as if I had been hit by a train but the only thing that was truly hurt and injured was my heart. I called Demetri but I could barely even talk through my sobs. He told me he would be on his way to see exactly what was going on since he really couldn't understand me over the phone. I put on a shirt and a pair of jogging pants so I wouldn't still be butt ass naked when Demetri arrived. He was knocking on my door about 15 minutes later, but the door was still unlocked so he let himself in.

"What's going on bro?"

"She left me man. For the first time in my life I was faithful and committed and she left me", I said with my face buried in my hands.

"What happened?" Demetri took a seat across from me on the sofa.

“Man, Tasha brought her ass over here while I was in the shower and pretty much tried to fuck me then Kendra walked in and caught us but I didn't fuck her despite what it looked like.”

“How did she get in here in the first place?” Of course the lawyer in him was going to bombard me with 21 questions.

“I left the door unlocked because Kendra lost her keys and I didn't want to hop out the shower to open the door for her but Tasha crazy ass been stalking me. I never let her come to my crib before. I always went to her place. She did this shit on purpose!” I threw the TV remote across the room out of frustration.

“So, I'm guessing Kendra gave you that black eye too?”

“Yeah, she punched the shit out of me! I didn't know she had it in her. I'm lucky to still be breathing based off the way she looked at me. She wanted to kill me bro for real”, I stated as I paced back and forth in the living room.

“I mean she does lift weights for a living so I'm pretty sure she can pack one hell of a punch”, Demetri chuckled to lighten the mood, but I couldn't laugh.

“Is she at your house with Kelsey?” I stopped pacing to look him the eye and see if he would lie to cover for Kelsey.

“She wasn't there when I left, but if she shows up I'll let you know. Just give her some space for now.”

“No, I'm not giving her space because the more time she has to think, the less likely she'll want to listen to me and work it out.” I started pacing back and forth again.

“So what do you plan on doing?”

“First, I'm going to her job to see if I can talk to her. If that doesn't work then I'll wait outside her place every night until she talks to me. I can't just sit back and not do anything bro.” My voice was starting to crack but I refused to cry in front of him.

“Yeah, I understand. I have to get back to the crib to check on my girls but I'll call if Kendra’s there. Call me if you need me bro”, he announced as he stood to leave.

“I wish I could check on my girl.” I buried my face back in my hands.

“Lock the door bro. I'll talk to you later.”

I sat in that same spot for hours deep in thought. I had probably called Kendra a hundred times by now and each time it went straight to voicemail. I was going crazy wondering what she was doing and if she was with another man. I didn't sleep at all and I called in for work because I'd be damn if I showed up and have to explain how my girl gave me a black eye. The next morning I went to her job where they informed me that she had temporarily transferred to another gym but they weren't liable to disclose which gym it was. I went to her apartment every day after that since and I had yet to catch up with her. Days slowly dragged by as she ignored any form of communication with me day in and day out. Now it had been weeks since I'd seen her, touched her, made love to her, or heard her laugh and it was driving me crazy. We were supposed to be planning our wedding and now I was on the brink of depression trying to get my girl back. I went to the bar every night after work and temporarily drank my problems away. It was funny how I had fallen in love and now I was at the bar getting drunk, falling apart each day. I wanted to meet the person stupid enough to invent this shit called love. I was quickly learning that love must not love anyone if this was the type of pain it caused. This was the type of pain that couldn't be healed with medicine or covered up with a Band-Aid. This pain was something you could only feel and not touch. It tore me to pieces so much that I was only a shell of myself. It was the weekend and I didn't plan on doing anything or going anywhere. All I wanted to do was lay in bed with my blinds closed repeatedly listening to K-Ci and Jojo's song "Crazy". Kendra was still ignoring me and I had pretty much tried everything that I could think of to reach her. I honestly didn't know what else to do so I decided to just give her time. I wondered if she ever thought about me and if she missed me as much as I'm missing her right now.

Chapter Thirteen:

Kendra

"Oh my God Kelsey I feel like I've been hit by a car!" I yelled in between sobs. I had my head resting on Kelsey's lap as I cried my eyes out. She came to visit me at the hotel I'd been staying at because I didn't want to be anywhere near Marcus. If I see him I might kill him and I refuse to end up like my mother.

"How about you try talking to him? You never gave him a chance to explain and I think you should at least hear what he has to say. Plus, I don't think Marcus is dumb enough to give you keys to his place to let you catch him cheating. That isn't logical", Kelsey pleaded.

"Men aren't logical and neither is love. I was doing just fine without him in my life", I sniffed and wiped the snot that was escaping my nostrils.

“No you weren't so be honest with yourself. I think he should know that you're pregnant Kendra. Don’t be selfish and not allow him to enjoy pregnancy with you. If you guys are together or not you still have to communicate for the baby's sake.”

“I don't even know how this happened! As much as we have sex, we always use protection and I'm on birth control. I just can't see him right now Kelsey.”

“So what are you going to do about the wedding?”

“I honestly haven't thought about the wedding. I'm more concerned about the baby.” I sat up from her lap and slouched on the sofa.

“How far along are you again?”

“I'm eight weeks right now.”

“If you don't tell him I will”, Kelsey said with conviction.

“Damn so it’s like that?”

“Yeah, it is because he deserves to know so stop being stubborn and talk to him. From what I hear, Demetri said he's deep in depression right now. Is that how you want to end things with him?” I hate it when she tries to be the voice of reason because she’s usually right, but my stubbornness was something serious. She should know that about me by now.

“I want him to hurt as much as I'm hurting. Is that so wrong?”

“It is if you don't know if he actually cheated and you're keeping your pregnancy from him.”

“Damn Kelsey whose side are you on because it really sounds like you're team Marcus right now?” I was starting to get irritated and frustrated because I knew she was right but I still didn’t want to accept the truth that maybe I overreacted.

“The only side I'm on is the logical side. It makes no sense for Marcus to have another woman in his house that you have keys to and he was expecting you home from work. Do you need me to break it down to you even more Kendra? Let's be realistic for a second, if Marcus wanted to cheat on you he would have gotten a hotel instead of bringing a woman to the apartment that you practically live in. Need I say more?” Kelsey stated in a matter of fact tone which made me feel so stupid.

“I get it Kelsey. I'm not stupid. If the shoe were on the other foot, what would you have done?”

“Honestly, I would have thrown that trick out of our house and then had a heart-to-heart with him to see if it was worth salvaging and to at least give him an opportunity to explain his side of the story." Ugh, I hate it when she's right!

"I guess I owe him that much. I just had to get away before I caught a case. I love my freedom too much to be locked behind bars over some foolishness."

"I totally understand, but the least you can do is give him a call. He's been worried sick about you."

"No, I rather talk to him in person because I can tell when he's lying and he's usually lying about something stupid. He does this cute thing with his nose every time he lies. It never fails. I miss him so much and I been horny like crazy. We've never gone this long without sex." These pregnancy hormones have my sex drive doing numbers. I would be lying if I said I didn't miss having sex with Marcus.

"Well, I did what I came here to do. I had to talk some sense into you because I know Marcus wouldn't disrespect you like that. Now, go home and talk to him. I'm getting tired of coming to this hotel to see you anyway."

"I plan on checking out tonight and going home. Where's my niece anyway?"

“She's at home with her daddy being spoiled by him as usual. He'll regret it when she gets older.”

“You know you spoil her too so stop fronting.”

“Of course I do, but he goes overboard and you know that.”

“Okay maybe he does go overboard just a tad bit”, I laughed with her.

“Come on, I'll help you pack so you can finally go back home to your man because I know you got some cobwebs brewing down there”, Kelsey laughed as she stood.

“Oh you got jokes, huh? Let's not forget who the queen of cobwebs really is!”

We joked back and forth with one another and packed my belongings. I can't deny that I have been missing Marcus like crazy. I missed his touch, his scent, and his funny sense of humor. It was hard for me to be mad at him for some reason. I didn't want to admit it to myself but I really wanted to see him and be around him. After Kelsey left, I checked out of the hotel and made my way to his apartment. I was nervous and excited to see him. I didn't know how I wanted to approach the conversation that we desperately needed to have. Should I be stubborn with him and not show any emotion or should I wear my emotions on my sleeve and be vulnerable? He didn't know I was coming and I kind of wanted to do a pop-up visit to see what was really going on. I still didn't have my keys so I put my suitcases down and knocked on his door. It took him a while to answer but when he opened the door he was shocked and happy to see me. He immediately embraced me.

"Baby, I'm sorry. I really am. Don't ever leave me without giving me a chance to explain. Just don't ever leave me like that again." He kissed me on my lips and my body responded to his touch. Did I mention how much I missed this?

"I'm sorry too. I should have given you the opportunity to explain what happened, but if I would have stayed any longer I don't know what I would have done." I made eye contact with him and his stare penetrated my soul. He always had a way of seeing beyond my tough exterior.

"You couldn't respond to my calls or text messages though?"

"I just needed some space Marcus."

"I want you to know that I didn't touch her. I left the door open for you while I took a shower. When I got out, she was sitting on the sofa. Apparently, she had been stalking me for months because she's never been to my place until that day. I tried to put her out and that's when you came in. I know what it may have looked like with me being naked and all but I didn't fuck her, I didn't touch her, and I did nothing wrong. You have to believe me." His eyes pleaded for me to understand where he was coming from.

I looked him in the eyes and I believed everything he was saying to me without a doubt. He looked a little rough, like he hadn't shaved in a few weeks, but he still looked good as hell to me. My body was reacting to his presence. I still had to tell him about the pregnancy though.

"I believe you. I also have something to tell you." I looked down at my feet and twirled a strand of my hair because I was nervous even though I knew he loved me.

"What's that?" he asked, as he grabbed my suitcases and put them in the living room shutting the door behind him.

"I'm eight weeks pregnant."

"I really hope it's a girl!" he said smiling from ear to ear.

He picked me up and carried me to his bedroom. I knew he'd been just as horny as me because we both have a high sex drive. He laid me on the bed and started yanking my clothes off. I could tell by his actions he was sexually frustrated and the feeling was mutual. I laid naked on his bed and watched him take his shirt and jogging pants off. Marcus took his time kissing all over my body and being gentle with me. He was usually rough but it had been awhile so I understand that he wanted to cherish this moment. He buried his face in between my thighs and went to work sucking on my clit and licking all over me. I caressed the waves in his hair and encouraged him to keep doing what he was doing to me because I loved every minute of it. He pushed my legs back and dove his tongue deeper inside of me. The sensations had me gripping the sheets and moaning his name because I was about to come all over his face. He eased a finger inside of me and hooked it into a position that hit my "G" spot which made me come all over the place. I'd never been a squirter and I don't know what the hell he did to make my body react the way it did but I never came like that ever before. He didn't even give my body time to calm down from my orgasm before he crawled between my thighs and eased his dick inside of me. He couldn't help but moan when he entered me without a condom. This was the first time we didn't use protection and I felt him raw. He had me clenching the sheets again as I wrapped my legs around his waist because I wanted to feel all of him like I'd never felt him before. It felt like heaven when he stroked deeper and bit down on my shoulder. I dug my nails into his lower back and made him moan. I rolled him over on his back to ride him like a Thoroughbred and he already knew what was up once I climbed on top. He never pulled out so I kept the rhythm that he had started. I rolled my hips and grinded on his dick just the way he likes it. He gripped my hips and met my motions as I watched him bite down on his lower lip. He was making so many different faces and I could tell that he wouldn't be able to last much longer. I did his favorite thing of rubbing his balls while he's deep inside of me to send him over the edge. He gripped my hips tight and moaned several different curse words as he jerked inside of me. I stayed on top and kissed his lips. I could tell he had after-shock because he was stuck and didn't want me to move an inch as he continued to grip my hips. When he finally let go I climbed off of him, grabbed him by the hand and led him to the bathroom. It had been weeks since we had showered together and I missed it. He climbed in behind me and kissed my neck while his hands roamed all over my body and caressed the small baby bump that I was now sporting. We were all over each other in the shower exactly like we used to be while I enjoyed some back shots as the water trickled down my body. We were in there so long that the water eventually got cold. After using up all the hot water, we went back to his bedroom and fucked all over his dresser and in front of the mirror. For majority of the time, he actually watched himself in the mirror. His damn arrogance was hilarious to me but also so sexy. I fell right to sleep in the comfort of his embrace after our make-up sex. My pregnancy was really starting to drain all of my energy.

We were all over each other for the next few days making up for lost time. Instead of actually planning a wedding, we decided to go to Vegas to get married. We agreed that since we both didn't have much family, this was the best decision for us. After leaving Vegas, we flew to St. Thomas for our honeymoon. We stayed there for a week and enjoyed every minute of it. We rented a cabana and consummated our marriage over that beach house. We even made love on the beach during the wee hours of the morning which had always been a fantasy of mine. Once our honeymoon was over, it was back to Wisconsin and the bipolar weather. We finally bought a house together once we made it back home and immediately started decorating the nursery. We were both excited about parenthood.

Chapter Fourteen:

Kelsey

Lately, I hadn't been myself in front of Demetri and I could tell he was really worried about my mental state especially since he knew my history with depression. I hadn't told him about the nightmares I'd been having because I knew if I did, he'd probably become more paranoid than me. I'd been having the same nightmare that got progressively worse each and every night. It started with me running for my life in the middle of darkness but then it progressed to hearing a baby crying in the background as I continued to run in the middle of nowhere. The dreams would end with gunshots being fired and blood splattering everywhere before suddenly going pitch black into total darkness. There was no way I could to tell Demetri about this. Parts of me already felt that he thinks I was going crazy. Not being myself around him left me detached and sometimes aloof because I couldn't stop thinking about the dreams.

After leaving Kendra's hotel, my intuition led me to the public library to do some research. I wasn't quite sure exactly what I was looking for. I just knew that I needed answers. I don't know what came over me when I typed Karma's name in the Google search bar. Yes, I had a file on her at the office but I didn't dig deep into her background. Some articles about her career as a defense attorney popped up. I was just about to close the browser window when I noticed something interesting. It was an old newspaper article about the death of what seemed to be her biological parents. I clicked the link and read the article. Apparently, her parents were killed in a house fire that seemed to have some foul play that was never fully investigated. It read on to say that Karma was placed into state custody until she turned eighteen and rightfully inherited her parents' life insurance policy, which was calculated to be around 2.5 million dollars. Her parents were known as a prominent and prestigious couple. Her father was a successful defense attorney and her mother was a respected dentist. To my surprise, Karma was a Wisconsin native as well. I wondered if Demetri was aware of this. I printed out the news article and hid it inside my purse.

After leaving the library, I had a nagging feeling in the pit of my gut that wouldn't go away. For some reason, I felt as if Karma was somehow connected to my nightmares and not fully out of the picture like Demetri thought she was. I mean I did see her up close and personal for myself so I knew just how crazy she could be. When I made it home, Demetri was knocked out on the couch with Destiny fast asleep peacefully laying on his chest. I smiled at the sight of them and turned off the television before heading upstairs to hop in the shower. They were still sleeping when I got out so I gently picked up Destiny and took her upstairs to her nursery. I knew Demetri had been exhausted lately, mainly because of me, so I decided to let him be on the couch. I retreated to our bedroom and called it a night. I was in a deep slumber when the dream crept up on me again. I could feel my body jumping but I couldn't wake myself up. This dream was definitely more intense than the others had been. This one was more vivid and detailed. I was in the middle of what appeared to be a forest and I was running like my life depended on it. I looked totally out of character with bruises and blood on my face and body. I heard a baby scream at the top of its lungs as Destiny's face quickly flashed before my eyes when suddenly there was total darkness once again.

I jumped up from under the covers and ran to her room almost tripping myself. She wasn't in her crib where I left her sleeping. I was trying not to panic and lose my mind. I simply hoped that Demetri grabbed her for some daddy-daughter time but that theory was shattered when I ran downstairs to see him still knocked out and Destiny nowhere in sight. Now, I was about to lose it!

"Demetri wake up! Where is Destiny? I put her in the crib but she's not there!" I was running through our house checking every room for a sign of her.

"What the fuck do you mean she's not in her crib? The last thing I remember is her sleeping on my chest!" He never cursed at me or talked to me this way, but I understood his frustration because I wasn't myself at the moment either. I'll be damned if I let anything happen to my baby! I don't think my heart could bare that.

"I put her in her crib when I got home because you were sleeping. Then I went to sleep and had another nightmare. I ran to her room but she wasn't there!" I yelled at him as he ran to different rooms and grew more frantic. He picked up his cell phone and dialed 911. He told the operator what was going on and they informed us they would have someone on it right away. The next call he made was to Pops. They were just as frantic as we were and adamant about coming to see what the police was going to do about this. Both the police and Demetri's parents arrived at the same time. I was crying my eyes out and hysterical at this point. We were all huddled in the living room when the detectives introduced themselves. They were two white males who looked as if they served in the military based off of their haircuts. One of them was short and stocky while the other was short and skinny. They looked too young to be seasoned detectives in my opinion.

“I'm sorry we're meeting under such circumstances but I’m Detective Michael O’ Donnell and this is my partner Parker Collins. So, can you tell us what happened here tonight?” he asked with his pen and notepad ready.

“Well, I put our daughter in her nursery after I made it home. My husband was sleep so I put her down in her crib, took a shower, and then went to sleep myself. For some reason, I woke up out of my sleep to check on her and she was gone. My husband doesn't know where she is either so now we're here.” I left out the nightmare because I didn't want them to think I was crazy.

“Do you know of anyone who would want to harm you or your family?” asked Detective O'Donnell.

“Well, I do have a disgruntled ex-fiancée but I have a restraining order on her and I haven't had contact with her in over a year.” Demetri was frantic as he tried to keep it together.

“What is her name and place of employment? We'll check to see if she has anything to do with the disappearance of your daughter. Is there anyone else you could think of?" he asked as he continued scribbling his notes.

"Her name is Karma Watts and other than her, I don't know of anyone else." Demetri was practically in tears now.

"Okay, those are all the questions we have for now, and we'll keep you updated on the status of Miss Watts. That's pretty much all we could do as of right now." He stated as he tucked his notepad away inside his suit.

"That's it?" I was growing angry with these detectives. I could have done that shit myself.

"Yes, I'm sorry we can't be of more assistance right now but we will keep you updated. Thank you for your time."

"Thanks for nothing", I told detective O'Donnell.

The detectives left just as quickly as they had come and I was pissed. All they could do right now was ask questions?!?! Demetri was sitting on the sofa when he broke down crying. Ma went over to console him while Pops aimlessly looked out of the window. I don't know what had come over me but I was no longer the reserved, conservative wife and mother. I was a lioness on a mission to keep her cub safe by any means necessary and if that meant doing things out character, then so be it. I already knew that Demetri was going to do everything by the book because that was just his nature but I had something else in mind. I stood next to Pops and spoke to him in a low voice because I didn't want Demetri to know what I was up to.

“Pops I need a favor.”

“What's that?” He didn’t look at me probably because he already knew what was on my mind.

“I know you have friends in high places but I’m also hoping you have a few friends in low places as well. I need a couple of things”, I whispered as we both aimlessly looked out of the window.

“Of course I know people from the gutter. Shit, I’m from the gutter. I don't want to know what you're up to. The less I know, the better. I'll give you a contact who's been a good friend of mine since back in the day. I keep him out of jail so he owes me a few favors anyway. Whatever you need, whether it's legal or illegal, he can make it happen. I advise you to be careful though.” Pops pulled out his wallet and handed me a card with a number on it and the name Gee.

After Pops and Ma left, Demetri and I barely spoke. We were both deep and distraught in our own thoughts. Demetri was definitely more distraught than I was. Not because my baby's disappearance didn't affect me, I was just busy coming up with a plan to get her back because my gut told me that bitch Karma had a hand in this. I never told Demetri this but that gold, engraved bracelet I bought actually has a tiny tracking device hidden inside. There was one problem though; it could only pick up a signal whenever you were within a 25 foot radius. Knowing this calmed me just a tad bit. I knew that if I wanted to find Destiny, I just had to do my research on Karma and really dig into her childhood to find anything that could lead me to my baby.

The next morning, I paid a trip to the police department where Marcus worked even though I told Demetri I was going to the gym to clear my mind and relieve some stress. I had never lied to him before but this was something I had to do to protect him. I had also never used a gun before and had no clue how to work it, so I needed some favors from Marcus. I made it to his job and waited for him in his office since he was still stuck in a meeting. I was looking at a picture of him and Kendra that was posted front and center on his desk when he entered his office. Demetri had already told them about Destiny's disappearance and they were just as distraught as we were so whatever I needed, he was liable to make it happen.

“What's up sis, what can I do for you?” he asked as he took a seat at his desk.

“Well, I need a few things. For starters I need you to keep this conversation strictly between me and you because Demetri is already worried and I don't need him stressing out about what I have planned. I also need you to give me access to the case regarding the death of Karma’s parents.”

“You think she has something to do with this?” His eyebrows were raised and I had his undivided attention.

“No, I *know* she has something to do with this. I also need a bulletproof vest along with some target practice and gun lessons from a licensed professional. Can you make that happen like yesterday?”

“Come on now, you know you're talking to a man with all the plugs and connections right? Let me make a few calls first. As far as the file case for Karma’s parents, give me a minute and I'll be back with it.” I waited a few minutes before Marcus returned with the file.

“You got twenty four hours to keep this file but then I need it back before anyone notices it missing”, he said as he sat the box on his desk.

"That's more than enough time. What about my other request?"

"One of my frat brothers is going to meet you downtown at the gun range to help you with whatever you need and provide you with the vest as well. Be careful with that crazy bitch." His facial expression told me that he was concerned for my safety but he knew he couldn't say anything that would change my mind.

"I'm not worried whatsoever about her crazy ass. She needs to be worried about me. Thanks for the favors. I owe you one", I said as I grabbed the box and headed for the door.

"Don't worry about that. Just make sure my niece is safe."

"That's the plan. I'll talk to you soon."

After I left the police department, I made my way to the slums of the city to meet with Pop's connect. I was headed to Burleigh Zoo which was an urban area riddled with violence and crime. Even though I grew up in a suburban middle class neighborhood, there was no culture shock because I had spent so much time in this area with Kendra when we we're kids. My parents thought we were at the library when we were really just roaming the streets. I pulled into an alley as instructed by Gee and waited for someone to show up. I requested him to bring me a few things that I felt were necessary. I asked him to bring me a gun for a woman to carry that packed a punch and had a silencer connected, brass knuckles, and the strongest pepper spray available. I got out of my car and leaned on the passenger side when an all-black car with black tinted windows pulled into the alley. It stopped in front of me and a man rolled down the driver window. It was a dark-skinned brother with a low haircut, dark shades and a gold grill that decorated his mouth. His appearance had drug dealer written all over him.

"What's up Doc? I heard you need a few gifts so I'm here to deliver. You got my bread?" he asked as he took his shades off and looked me up and down with a grin plastered on his face.

"How much do you want?"

"Well because you look as good as you do, I'll give you a deal. I'll take $350 for everything since you fine as hell and you know my nigga." I handed him the cash and he handed me a brown paper bag filled with the items I requested.

"It was nice doing business with you baby. You should call me sometime." He smiled again and damn near blinded me with the sunlight hitting his grill and reflecting the diamonds in it.

“I'm happily married so no thank you. Have a nice day.” I hopped in my car and pulled off before he had a chance to respond with the typical “so you can’t have friends” line that most Milwaukee men use after rejection.

I went to the library to study the case file Marcus had given me. I went through a countless amount of paperwork with my eyes wide open for anything I could possibly use. I was about to give up when something caught my attention. Karma had a child psychologist when she was an adolescent. They evaluated her from age eight until her late teenage years. Apparently, her parents arranged for her to have a psychologist because of her bizarre, temperamental behavior. I had heard of this psychologist before. She was a well-respected child psychologist who was also a Wisconsin native that paved the way for other black, female psychologists. She was very involved in the community as an advocate to help rebuild the family structure in the black communities and she was quite the philanthropist. I admired her career and aspired to be like her as a child so it was an honor to actually meet her. The plan was to contact her and find out what I could about Karma’s past. From what I heard about Dr. Ellis Ross was that she was now retired and residing near the lake in Milwaukee, Wisconsin so hopefully it wouldn't be too difficult reaching her. I typed her name and occupation in the search engine and she instantly popped up. An office number was listed as her contact so I pulled out my cell phone and punched the numbers in my keypad. I waited a few moments and then a woman answered.

“Dr. Ross speaking, how may I help you?”

“Hi, Dr. Ross. My name is Dr. Smith Latimore and I'm calling on behalf of a former patient of yours by the name of Karma Watts. Do you by any chance remember anything significant about her childhood?”

“Yes, I remember Ms. Karma Watts very well. She was a very troubled soul. Are you currently her psychologist?”

“No, not currently but she was briefly one of my patients.”

“So what can I do for you?”

“I need to know everything significant that occurred in her childhood. Maybe a special place that she frequently retreated to or a family member that knows her current mannerisms that are relevant to her childhood.”

“I think it's best that we meet in person because I'd hate to give bad news over the phone. Are you in the Milwaukee area?”

“Yes I am actually. I can meet you at Carson’s restaurant downtown in about thirty minutes.”

“That'll work for me, and just to let you know what I look like if I make it there before you, I have long curly sisterlocks.”

“Alright, I'll see you soon.”

I made a phone call to Demetri on my way to Carson’s because it had been hours since I checked in with him. He was still distant and distraught. It was going on day two of Destiny being kidnapped and the detectives were still of no assistance. I'd come to the conclusion that this situation couldn't be handled by the book especially since my daughter’s life was on the line. I was going to be the judge, the jury, and the punisher in this case. I hated to break the news to Tristan since it was time for him to study for his college finals. I didn't want him to panic knowing how protective he was over our family. He was about to be on the next flight to Wisconsin when I convinced him not to come. I vowed to him that I would do everything in my power to find her and protect her. I told him about the tracking device to ease his nerves a bit and it seemed to work for the time being. I finally found a parking spot a block away from Carson's and walked to the restaurant. When I entered, I immediately spotted Dr. Ross sitting at a booth in the back of the restaurant. She was beautiful for a woman in her late sixties and her silver locks were gorgeous and neat. She waved for me to join her at the booth.

"Nice to formally meet you Dr. Ross", I said as I took a seat inside the booth.

"Likewise. So, there are some troubling things about Karma's childhood I should probably brief you on, but first I need to know why you're so interested in her past."

"I'll just be completely forthcoming with you. I'm married and I recently had a baby girl with my husband. My husband was engaged to Karma while I was her psychologist. I had known my husband from college, however, at the time of her being my patient I didn't know that she was engaged to him. As her psychologist, I was aware that she was unable to have children, but I never disclosed that information to my husband. He eventually learned that on his own which ended up being a deal-breaker for him and his relationship with her. The point is, my daughter has been missing for two days and I'm 100% sure that she has something to do with it since she was disgruntled with their separation and our child. So, I need every piece of information I can gather in order to find her because I refuse to tragically lose my daughter like I lost my first husband." I was on the brink of tears now.

"I understand, and I'm here to tell you that your intuition about her stands correct; she can be very vindictive and malicious when she doesn't get her way, even when she was a child. I've witnessed it firsthand, up close and personal on a number of occasions so I'm fully aware of her devious ways. Her parents were good friends of mine from college and they were well aware of her mental disorders. They did everything in their power to stabilize her mental state. However, she really started to rebel when she was prescribed medications to counter her behavior. She literally morphed into another person. Shortly after she was mandated to take her medications on a daily basis while being monitored doing so, her parents mysteriously died in a house fire. There was this place she constantly mentioned when she was a child. I believe it was some type of forest. If I recall correctly, the name of it is Kettle Moraine Forest. This was a safe haven for her. Her father took her on camping trips there during her childhood since they owned a piece of camping ground there. I hope this information can be some sort of assistance to you", she said with her eyebrows raised.

"Oh my gosh! It all makes sense now. Thank you for meeting me. I really do appreciate you for sharing this information." I stood and shook her hand as I was about to leave the restaurant.

"You're very welcome. Just be careful with this one because she is feisty", she stated with concern.

"Being feisty is no comparison to someone who's deadly when provoked. Thank you for the warning though."

"Best of luck to you Dr. Latimore."

"Thanks again."

After I left the restaurant, I headed to the police department to return the case file that Marcus let me borrow. Then I went home to spend some quality time with my husband since I was literally going to war that night. I didn't know if I would make it out of the trenches to see him again but I was on a mission to get my baby girl back. When I made it home the entire house was pitch black. I knew Demetri was here because his truck was in the driveway. I ran up the stairs two at a time and flicked on the lights in the hallway and in Destiny's nursery. Demetri was rocking in the rocking chair and holding her favorite blanket the she always cuddled with. Seeing him in so much pain and not being able to diminish it was genuinely killing me inside. I had finally healed from labor but we were yet to have sex because we were both mentally out of it. His eyes were bloodshot red as if he'd been crying all day and I could tell that he was mentally defeated. Not knowing if Destiny had been fed or taken care of like she was accustomed to frighten me and pissed me off even more inside.

I stood in front of Demetri, held his chin in my hand and looked into his hazel eyes. We hadn't spoken to each other much as of late, but the vibe we shared resulted in no words being necessary. I knew him so well. His body language was telling me that he needed love and affection. I straddled his lap and kissed him on the lips. I knew he wasn't craving sex. He was craving a shoulder to cry on. I had never seen him cry before this happened but it didn't make me question his masculinity. This actually made me respect him even more as a man. His head rested between my breasts as I consoled him by rubbing his back. I'm pretty sure he was experiencing the same pain I experienced with Tristan’s death, but this time I had a chance to get a different outcome and I would give my last breath to find her alive.

We stayed in this position for a while and just held each other. It was as if we were gathering strength from one another through our embrace. Not having Destiny around and seeing that beautiful smile made it obvious that we were missing a huge part of our puzzle. Without her we both felt incomplete. I grabbed him by the hand and lead him to the shower. After we took a shower together, we cuddled without really saying much. I honestly didn't know what to say to him anyways but his strong embrace was comforting enough to calm my nerves. I turned around to face him while I looked into those pretty hazel eyes that I'd grown obsessed with and just stared at him. I caressed the side of his check with my thumb and kissed him on the lips. I really felt the need to show him and tell him how much I love him. His eyes got lost in mine as he returned my gaze which was like words of affection. He surprised me when he climbed on top of me because I wasn't expecting him to be in the mood for sex. He skipped our usual foreplay and made love to me as if it was our last time seeing each other. Little did he know that could actually be the case in this instance.

After we made love I drifted off to sleep and the same dream I'd been having for the past few months crept up on me again. This was like the finale of all the dreams I had. The setting of the dream was still in a forest like environment, but this time there was a small cabin in the middle of nowhere hidden within the trees. I was still running as if my life depended on it but the reason why I was running was still unclear. There was a loud bang and I fell to the ground. A few moments after I fell, Karma hovered over me and pointed a gun in my face. I forced myself to wake up because I didn't want to know the end result of this dream. I glanced over at Demetri and surprisingly, he was still sleeping. I grabbed my phone and opened the app that was connected to the device in Destiny's bracelet but the connection was still nonexistent. I jumped out of bed and grabbed a piece of paper and pen to write Demetri a note for whenever he woke up. I simply wrote that I went for a run to clear my mind. I went to a spot in our walk-in closet down the hall where I hid all of my items for this altercation. I put on my bulletproof vest, black jogging pants, a loose fitting t-shirt, and a loose fitting black hoodie to hide the fact that I was wearing a vest. I put my hair in a tight bun and threw on the most comfortable pair of sneakers that I owned along with my brass knuckles that I got from Gee. I wore some open finger black gloves to cover the brass knuckles and hid the small can of pepper spray in my Nike sports bra just in case I needed it. Finally, I connected the silencer onto the gun that I was now an expert with and tucked it into the waistband of my jogging pants. It was still dark outside so I grabbed a flashlight to assist me in this journey of getting my baby back. I went back to the bedroom and checked on Demetri one last time before I left. I could tell that he was in a deep slumber because he'll usually wake up whenever I wasn't sleeping next to him. He looked so peaceful and of course handsome even as he slobbered on the pillow. I leaned in and kissed him on the forehead just before leaving the house.

I opened the tracking app on my phone again as I pulled out of our driveway. There was still no connection to the tracking device. I hopped on I-41 North and headed to a destination that was unfamiliar to me but I had faith in my intuition and my intelligence on Karma's state of mind. I'd been studying behavior patterns and analyzing them to predict future behaviors ever since I was in college so I was confident that my research would lead me to the right place. People don't realize that you can easily predict someone's next move by simply putting yourself in their shoes and leaving all preconceived notions at the door. There was still a chance that my child was still breathing but time was definitely against me so I had the pedal to the metal as I sped down I-41. There was literally no one else on the freeway which meant no traffic or lurking police. I was about 20 minutes into my drive to Kettle Moraine Forest when my phone lit up with a notification informing me that I was getting close to the vicinity of the tracking device. My adrenaline immediately began to rush through my veins along with a mixture of emotions. What if I were to finally get close to Destiny only to find her dead remains? What if Karma figured out that the bracelet was actually a tracking device and threw it out in the forest? She's intelligent and crazy enough to be as paranoid as I'd been lately. She had probably been on her toes just like I was, I rationalized with myself. I decided that in order to get through this altercation I had to force all doubt and hypothetical questions out of mind and replace them with thoughts of determination and a cold heart. I said a prayer to my Heavenly Father that I would find my daughter safe, soundly and hopefully in one piece.

I drove about another 10 minutes when my phone lit up with another notification showing that I was now over 1,500 feet in the vicinity of the tracking device. I pulled my car over but all I seen was trees everywhere. I grabbed my flashlight out of my purse and turned it on since the sun was nowhere near rising. I decided to take an educated guess and head north into the forest which just seemed like the most logical choice. Walking through the Forest was like deja'vu. It seemed so familiar because of the dreams that I had been experiencing every night. My phone lit up with another update. I was now almost within a thousand feet of the device. I was still a ball of emotions but if I wanted Destiny back I had to have an "I don't give a fuck/go hard or go home" attitude. I couldn't fight crazy from a logical standpoint. All common regard for human life was out of the window. My phone lit up again but this time it notified me that my phone no longer had signal. Damn I lost the connection to the device! Sprint's cellular signal always fucks up at the wrong time! I kept a fast pace and continued making my way through the forest to see if I could find a signal somehow. I was about to take my battery out of my phone and try to restart it when I heard a baby scream. I immediately dropped the cell phone and ran into the direction of the screams as fast as I could. I knew Destiny was frightened because she barely cried let alone screamed. My heart was pumping a mile a minute as I ran through the forest dodging branches and ditches with a vengeance. I finally noticed a small cabin a few hundred feet away when my fight or flight mode kicked in. Flight was not an option. I was in this shit for the fight. I had fist fights before back in the day but this was something totally different. This was an innocent life on the line because a crazy bitch couldn't get her emotions in check and move on.

When I finally reached the small cabin I noticed that it was dark except for a small lamp providing light in what appeared to be the living room. I could see a little bit through a side window of the cabin. I could also still hear Destiny screaming at the top of her lungs. I had to make a spilt decision on whether or not I wanted this to be a surprise attack or if I should make myself vulnerable by announcing my presence. I kneeled down and peeped in the window to figure out my next move but it was already decided for me when I see that Karma had a pillow over Destiny's face and was trying to smother her on the living room floor. Destiny was turning blue in the face. I ran my ass to the front of that cabin and kicked the front door in. Her eyes were wide with confusion when she looked up and seen me. I didn't give her a chance to react before I kicked her with all my might on the side of her head to stop her from smothering my baby to death. Destiny was still crying but I couldn't stop to check on her because I was in the zone. Karma fell on her side from the blow and I immediately pounced on her. I had my brass knuckles on when I punched her in her mouth and knocked her front teeth out. She yelled in agony and tried to block my blows. I was still throwing punches to her face when she picked up a vase and knocked me on the side of my head with it. This vase dazed me for a second since it shattered against my temple. I stopped my attack to nurture the blood that was oozing from the side of my head.

She pushed me down, crawled on top of me and wrapped her hands around my neck. I was still dazed and a little disoriented from the blow to my temple. She literally looked like a woman possessed by a demonic spirit. There was no life and no soul behind the possessive stare of her eyes. I was staring into the eyes of a woman that may have been normal at some point in her life but now she seemed as if she was consumed by evil. Her grip around my neck grew tighter and threatened to cut off my oxygen supply.

"This will teach you not to steal someone else's man you dumb ass bitch! You thought I was gonna let that shit slide?" she snarled through missing teeth as the hold on my neck grew tighter than before.

I was literally at a point where I couldn't breathe anymore but I suddenly remembered that I had that small can of pepper spray in my sports bra. I maneuvered my right hand from under her while she was preoccupied with choking the fucking life out of me and sprayed pepper spray directly in her eyes but it was so strong that it affected me too. I started coughing uncontrollably as if I was about to cough up a lung. She screamed and instantly starting rubbing her eyes. I pushed her off of me but before I could move she kicked me hard as hell in my ribs. I was really winded now. The sharp pain that paralyzed my body felt as if my ribs were either fractured or broken. I was hunched over on my knees trying to catch my breath when she kicked me in the same spot again. I yelled out in agony. If my ribs weren't broken at first, they damn sure were broken now. Her eyes were still bloodshot red from the pepper spray but that didn't deter her from attacking me. I gathered some energy to get through the pain of trying to stand up as she made her way over to where Destiny was still lying on the ground. As she pulled out a gun my heart skipped a beat. She looked at me while she pointed the gun back and forth at Destiny and me.

"I hate that this story doesn't have a happily ever after for you and Demetri. On second thought, I lied! I *love* the fact that this story will be a nightmare for you two! You thought you outsmarted me by getting pregnant by my man didn't you? I *always* get what I want and once you and this baby are out of the picture, I'll get my man and my life back. Now sit your ass down on that couch and don't move a fucking muscle! I want you to see the fate you've sealed for your precious little child before you die", she yelled through missing teeth and a bloody mouth which made her talk weird.

I played the role she wanted me to play and let her assume that I was helpless. I was taking huge a risk though because she could have easily killed me or Destiny at any moment but I knew this wasn't Karma talking. This was her alter ego Sassy in charge right now; the same personality that was in charge when Karma's parents were lit on fire. Taking those medications meant that her alter ego could no longer consume or live through her. I could tell that Sassy was the type to tell you everything she planned to do before she actually did it because she's arrogant like that. If she wanted to beat you in a sport, she'd be the type to rub it in your face and then tell you how she beat you and why you'll never be able to beat her. I used this knowledge to my advantage and let her sulk in what she thought was a victory. I sat on the couch as instructed while she rambled on and on about how she had been trailing us for months and how she kidnapped Destiny without any detection. While she was bragging on and on, I clicked off the safety on the gun and cocked it so it would be ready when I needed it.

I knew that I had to do something while she was ranting because if I didn't, she was just going to kill us both as soon as she was satisfied with her so-called victory speech. Again I was taking another major risk but I was more than willing to die trying to protect my child. Besides, I knew she still wasn't aware that I was wearing a bulletproof vest. I figured that any sudden movements would most likely get her attention so I quickly jumped up from the couch and lunged at her. She pointed the gun towards me and pulled the trigger. She shot me exactly where I thought she would, directly in the chest where I was protected by the bulletproof vest. The impact was still powerful. It felt as if I had taken a thousand punches to the chest all at once. The impact was so powerful that it knocked me off my feet and I fell on the floor next to the couch. I laid there as still as possible hoping to convince her that I was dead. This crazy bitch had the nerve to laugh as if she was watching a comedy show or something. She didn't check to see if I was dead. Once I heard her laugh, I figured she wouldn't. I was relieved that my assumptions for this scenario were going as planned. I told you that you could predict another person's future behaviors by analyzing them and mentally placing yourself in their thought process. I could safely say that her next move would be to literally talk to Destiny as if she could comprehend her. Once again, I knew that arrogant Sassy would tell Destiny what she planned on doing next. She was in the middle of raving about how strong Destiny was because she was still surviving even though she hadn't had anything to eat in days. That's when I made an acute and swift movement of taking my gun from my waistband and aiming it at her head. From my target practice, I knew I wasn't going to miss. I placed my index finger on the trigger just as she was about to aim her gun at Destiny and pulled it. The gun responded to my touch and silently fired one shot to the side of her temple.

Blood splatter and brain fragments flew everywhere and decorated the walls. I crawled over to Destiny to see if she was still breathing because she had stopped crying a long time ago. My ribs were swollen and in pain but I managed to get to her. I cried when I felt a pulse. It was a weak pulse but she was still alive and I thanked the Most High for that. I needed to get her to the hospital for some nutrition and to get her vitals back to normal because I could tell that she had lost some weight. I limped to the bedroom and pulled a sheet off the bed. I used the sheet to wrap Destiny around my body since I wasn't able to carry her. I had learned this technique from one of my patients who was from Africa and knowing it had finally come in handy. I wrapped Destiny in front of me and secured the sheet while avoiding my ribs all at the same time. When I felt she was secure, I limped my way to the front door and looked down at Karma's lifeless body.

"Karma's a bitch ain't it?" I said to her as I stepped over her body and exited the cabin.

I looked in the sky and simply said thank you to whomever was watching over us. I noticed red and blue lights flashing in the distance. I followed their direction just as the sun was starting to peak. It took me longer than normal to get there but when I did I was surprised to see an ambulance on the scene next to my car. I was even more shocked to see who was seated in the front of the police squad car. How did Demetri know where I was and what I was up to? When he noticed me he rushed out of the car and ran to me. He unwrapped Destiny from my chest, kissed her and held her close until he noticed that she was unresponsive. He called for the paramedics to take her and evaluate her. They took her out his hands and immediately started working on her. He tried to hug me but stopped when he seen me clutching my ribs.

"How did you know where I was Demetri?" I barely got the words out as a sharp pain ripped through my body.

"I woke up in the middle of the night and read the note you left but I know you wouldn't go for a jog outside while it was still dark. I called everyone and they said they hadn't spoken to you so I started to panic until I remembered you had OnStar installed in your car. I called them up and this is where they located you. I figured you probably had been digging up research on Karma but I didn't want to assume or want you to feel like I thought you were crazy. I'm just praying that my two favorite girls are going to be okay." He leaned in to kiss me on my forehead while he caressed my elbows since everything else on my body was either bruised or covered in blood.

"Great minds think alike", I smiled at him. I was grateful to be blessed with someone who was pretty much my other half. Everything that I was he was a reflection of and that's rare.

"Yeah and thank God for that", he smiled back at me. That natural attraction and vibe between us was still there. Our assigned case detectives approached me to conduct their investigation.

"In case you forgot, I'm Detective O'Donnell and this is my partner Detective Collins. Can you tell us what happened here tonight?" He had his pen and pad ready as if he was going to really do something with it.

"I think what you really mean is can you do my job for me again because I'm not competent enough to do it on my own? I think you know what happened here tonight if I'm standing here broken and bruised and covered in someone else's blood. It's called investigate and follow up on a hunch, right? It's something you two *should* know very well, but obviously don't", I said with sarcasm dripping from my tone.

"I understand that you're upset ma'am but it's important for us to take your statement while it's still fresh if you don't mind?" said Detective O'Donnell.

"Well, your best bet is to come to the hospital where I'll be treated for my injuries. I'm not stepping foot in a police station anytime soon!" I declared as I limped over to the ambulance. Demetri was just about to join me when his cell phone rang. I noticed the sudden changes of his facial expressions and I could tell that something was seriously wrong.

"What's going on babe?"

"That was Marcus. He's a little distraught because Kendra is going into labor right now. He wants me to meet him at St. Joseph's hospital. Do you want to get treated there so that we can all be under the same roof?"

"Yeah we can do that as long as Destiny is in good hands."

Demetri helped me get inside the ambulance with Destiny as we rushed to the hospital. The emergency personnel told us that she was unresponsive because she was in a coma. I couldn't believe what I was hearing but I was still grateful that she was still alive and breathing on her own. I was placed in a wheelchair and wheeled into the entrance when we made it to the hospital. Marcus spotted us and rushed over to Demetri and me. He embraced Demetri which surprised me because just like most men they never showed emotion to one another, but I understood why these circumstances were different. Destiny and I were taken to a room to be treated for our injuries while Marcus and Demetri went to the second floor where Kendra was being prepped for labor. I was in more pain than I'd ever experienced in my life. The doctors informed that it would take months for my ribs to heal because they were indeed broken. Destiny was hooked up to an IV to get her vitals back to normal and placed in an incubator next to me. I stared at her while she slept. She was still in a coma and the length of her coma was undetermined. The doctor said that she had suffered from malnutrition and a head injury but she shocked them because she was very strong to be an infant. I would go through this pain all over again just to protect her. I wouldn't change that for anything in the world. The doctors had given me a high dose of morphine to relieve some of the pain I was enduring so I eventually dozed off to sleep.

When I finally woke up I looked over to see if Destiny was still in her incubator but she wasn't there anymore. I was about to yank the IV out of my arm and search for her until Tristan came around from the other side of the curtain with her in his arms. Surprisingly, she was awake and smiling.

"How long have I been asleep?"

"Relax, Ma. I just got here and she was awake and crying so I picked her up. Man, she looks just like Pops. That's crazy! How are you feeling? I hope you feel better than you look right now?"

"I told you to stay your tail in Kentucky but I'll be better in time. Destiny is safe and that's all that matters", I stated as I tried to get comfortable on the lumpy hospital bed.

"Pops told me that you went gangster on ole girl. Where did you get a gun and bulletproof vest from anyway?" he asked as he twirled Destiny's fingers around his.

"Just know that I know people who know people. I would have done the same for you too. I don't play about my babies."

"I'm a grown man now, Ma."

"Even when you get old as dirt you still gon' be my baby. Was Destiny awake when you came here because the doctors said she was in a coma before I dozed off?"

"Yeah she was up when I made it here. They tried to give her some breast milk but she refused it. I think she could tell that it wasn't yours. You think you can breastfeed with your injuries?"

"Yeah, I can. I'm still doped up so I'm not in much pain right now." Tristan brought her close to me and propped her up so that I was able to feed her. She immediately latched on and started sucking. I wondered if the medication I was on would affect her. That's something I would have to ask the doctor but right now my baby girl was starving so I didn't have much of a choice but to breastfeed her. I was looking down at her and glaring into her hazel eyes when Demetri walked in. Every time I see him is like seeing him for the time. I still felt butterflies in the pit of my stomach whenever I seen him. We made eye contact with one another and smiled at the same time. He was looking good as ever even in a simple hoodie and jogging pants. He embraced Tristan then took a seat on the bed next to me and Destiny before wrapping his arms around us.

"I love you so much", he whispered as he leaned his forehead against mine.

"I love you too."

“I'm blessed because I have the things that money can't buy. I have a beautiful family and I couldn't ask for more.” It was nice to see his sensitive side because he usually tries to hide it.

“I'm blessed to see another day. I thought I was going to lose my life tonight. It was so worth the try though”, I said as I looked down at Destiny and smiled.”

“Yeah, you shocked me! I didn't know you had that fire in you”, Demetri laughed.

“Don't let my calm and collected demeanor fool you. I can handle my own baby”, I smiled back.

“Yeah, that makes you an O.G now Ma”, Tristan laughed.

“What's an O.G?” I was confused, maybe it was the meds.

“It's an abbreviation for original gangster. I forgot you don't know slang that well”, said Tristan.

“Oh, I knew that. Did Kendra have the baby yet?”

“Yeah they had a baby girl. Her name is Riley Love. Kendra was going crazy too”, said Demetri.

“What do you mean she was going crazy?”

“I mean she was yelling and screaming at the top of her lungs. She begged the nurses to give her all the medications they had available to ease her pain. Marcus tried to calm her down but he was just as stressed as she was. She was nothing like you during labor”, Demetri laughed.

“I knew she was going to change her mind about doing a natural birth. Everyone isn't built for that.” I had to laugh because I could only imagine how Kendra was acting upstairs.

“Marcus is going to bring her down here soon so you can see her. I’ve never seen him so excited before.”

“It's crazy how much he’s changed. I'm still shocked.”

“Yeah, I know right. I remember how he used to clown me for being a one woman man. Meeting the right person can change you for the better or the worst. Thankfully in his case it's clearly for the better.”

“I hear y'all talking smack about me”, Marcus announced as he walked in the room holding the newest edition to the family.

“Oh she is so gorgeous! Let me hold her”, I said as I handed Destiny to Demetri.

“She looks just like me right?”

“Yeah, she does but I can tell she’s going to take after Kendra's hair. Her hair is thick and full already”, I claimed.

“Yeah, I agree. I already feel older now that I'm a father. Things are changing for the better and when she gets old enough to date I'll be waiting for the dude with a shotgun!” Marcus laughed.

“Hell yeah and I’ll be right next to you with my gun just waiting for the nappy headed boy. It’s gonna be Bad Boys II all over again!” Demetri joked as they dabbed each other.

“I hate to break up y'all ‘“bromance”’, but how is Kendra doing Marcus?”

“She's knocked out from the meds she was given and I'm happy she is because she was really stressing me out with her antics during labor. I don't know if I can relive that again. Riley may be our only child”, Marcus laughed.

“Don't front on my girl like that. Imagine how you’d feel if you had to push out a 7 pound baby whether you were ready or not?”

“I'm not about the life so I can't even tell you.” Marcus was always in a joking mood. No matter what, he'd always make you laugh. There was a knock at the door.

“Come in”, I yelled. It was Pops and Mama at the door.

“How are you feeling baby girl?” Ma asked and she embraced me and kissed me on the cheek.

“I'm a little doped up right now but it's easing my pain. Four of my ribs are broken but I'm alive so I can't complain.”

“You two are alive and well and that's all that matters. Now hand me my princess I missed her so much.” There was another knock at the door. It was the detectives from earlier. Ma handed Destiny back to Demetri and left us to talk with the detectives.

“Can we have a moment of your time to take your statement?” asked Detective O’Donnell.

“Sure.” My response was dry because I didn't care to do their job for them again. Everyone left the room except for Demetri and Pops just in case I needed any legal advice.

“I understand that you may not be up to talking right now but as I stated before it's important to take your statement while everything is still fresh.”

"I understand. What happened is I paid a visit to Karma's child psychologist who told me about a forest that her father owned a piece of land on so I went to the cabin that she spoke about and I found Karma there in the middle of smothering my child. I ran into to cabin and stopped her from smothering my daughter. She shot me but I came prepared with a bulletproof vest and I returned a single shot to her temple. That's what happened." I gave them the edited version because I didn't care to go into every single detail. It was their job to figure out the details, not mine.

"What made you visit the forest in the middle of the night and how did you know she had your child?" O'Donnell inquired.

"It's called intuition and pure intelligence. I've been studying behaviors for years and this situation was no different from any other patient I've analyzed."

"So you came prepared to her property for an altercation? This sounds like premeditated murder in my opinion", said detective Collins.

"Be careful with that murder word there, detective. First degree murder will never stand in court with all of the physical evidence stating otherwise. I would tread lightly if I were you, especially if you want to keep your badge", claimed Pops.

“Is this an interrogation or a simple conversation to gather a statement?” inquired Demetri.

“This is just a simple conversation. Please forgive my partner. He was just speaking out of turn.” Detective O’Donnell shot a dirty look to Detective Collins.

“Let's just get to the matter at hand. Is my client being charged with anything?” asked Pops.

“That has yet to be determined because we're still gathering all of the evidence from the crime scene. We'll keep you updated on that matter. Have a good night.” said detective O’Donnell as he inched his way to the door.

“What type of people are they hiring to be detectives these days? I can do better than them”, Pops bragged.

“You think you're good at everything anyways Pops”, laughed Demetri.

“That's because I am and that's not my fault. But if they try to charge you with anything, I’ll completely dismantle their case. They don't want me to show my ass in court. I’ll hurt their feelings”, said Pops.

“We all know that you're a beast in the courtroom. You don't have to brag”, Demetri laughed.

“I'm just saying that they don't want these problems. Speaking of work, I got some stuff to handle so I gotta run but if you need me Kelsey you know my number”, he said as he gathered his things to leave.

“Don't worry Pops, if she's in my hands then she’s in good hands. I learned from the best. Tell Ma that I'll call her later.”

“Damn, right! I'll see y'all later”, exclaimed Pops.

“See you later”, I said to Pops.

“So how are you feeling?” Demetri turned his attention to me.

“I may need another dose of meds because my pain is increasing in my side again.”

I called in the nurse to give me some more medication. Destiny was now fast asleep in the incubator when I glanced over at her. Demetri cuddled up next to me as best as he could without hurting my ribs. It felt as if everything was back to normal except for the fact that we both had to heal from our wounds. I eventually dozed off from the medicine and for the first time in months I didn't have any nightmares.

Chapter Fifteen:

Tristan

It had been months since the incident and my mama was healing well. There were no charges filed against her since it was a clear case of self-defense. With the evidence of their restraining order against Karma and the history of her mental state, it was made very clear exactly who the aggressor was. I took the rest of the semester off after basketball season ended to help around the house since Demetri had to return to work. Destiny was back to her bubbly self and getting bigger each day. She was almost a year old now. I took a medical leave from school but I planned on returning for summer school to make up for the credits I was going to miss. Being in college and trying to hold on to my virginity was becoming more and more of a challenge every day on campus. It was a lot easier in high school because the majority of those girls were too immature for my liking anyway, but now I was faced with a variety of women. It was like being a kid in a candy store. I tried to occupy my time with school, working out, and attending church whenever I was back at home but I could only do that for so long.

It was about time for me to start summer school when I returned back to campus. I was actually excited because I had never been to summer school and being that it was outside of Wisconsin and on an exciting campus made me anxious to see what the night life had to offer. I had always been all work and no play so I was looking forward to going out with some of the players on the team. We were invited by a few cheerleaders to come to a party at a club near campus so I was more than excited to go. I was getting ready for the party back at the dorm that I shared with my roommate Troy, who was one of my boys from high school. We had both hooped together on the high school team. I had just come from the barbershop so I was low-key feeling myself. I was in my closet trying to find something to wear. My wardrobe usually consisted of jogging pants and hoodies but I had recently gone shopping to upgrade from my sports attire. I decided on a simple navy blue Ralph Lauren button up, some jeans and navy blue Nikes. I put on my best cologne and was brushing my hair as I looked at the image staring back at me in the mirror.

I was a spitting image of my dad and he would definitely be proud of me right now.

I was in my car with Troy and some other players from the team on our way to the party. The parking lot was packed so I assumed the party was going to be lit. They were all bragging about how many girls they were going to get and take back home while I was just hoping that I would find someone appealing since I was so selective when it came to the opposite sex. I was daydreaming when Troy snapped me out of it as I searched for a parking spot.

"Aye bro you got some gum or some breath mints or something?"

"No, nigga you should have brushed your teeth like I did", I joked with him.

"I did brush my teeth. I just want some extra protection because I'm mingling with all the chicks tonight", he smiled as he rubbed his palms together in anticipation.

"Well, you out of luck because I don't have any gum or breath mints."

"Take me to the gas station real quick then."

"Dude, why did you wait for me to get here to tell me that? You know how many gas stations I passed on my way here?" Troy and I always bickered with one another because he was more like my brother than my friend. We had been playing ball together since we were toddlers in AAU and had seen each other grow from boys to men.

"Well my breath wasn't feeling tart then so stop complaining. You know I got you on gas money bro."

"Man you still owe me from last time!"

"You know I'm a struggling college student. Everybody ain't rich like you!" Troy joked.

"Nigga I'm not rich! My mama work just like everyone else", I claimed as I pulled up to the gas station.

"You got yo own crib behind yo mama crib. If that ain't rich then I don't know what is", he laughed as he unbuckled his seatbelt.

"Shut up fool and bring me some gum too while you at it", I demanded as I put my car in park.

"Alright but I'm deducting that from the gas money I owe you."

"Wow, 75 cents is really going to put a dent in what you owe me", I laughed.

"You know every penny counts", he claimed as he slammed my door. He had a very bad habit of doing that.

He ran inside the gas station and bought some *Tic-Tacs* and gum. I chuckled to myself because this scene reminded me of one of my favorite movies, "*The Wood*", except we weren't caught in the middle of a robbery. I drove back to the club and still couldn't find a parking spot so I parked a few blocks away. The line for the party was wrapped around the block when we finally got closer to the club. I was trying to hide my anxiousness but I had to admit that I was geeked. I had never been to a club before because I never really had the time but I was feeling the atmosphere so far. All my boys and I were single so you know they were acting like dogs in heat when we finally paid the admissions fee and strutted in. The inside of the club was really dope. It was setup like a lounge but it also had a dance floor and the DJ was actually playing good music. Troy had a fake I.D so he was able to buy some shots from the bar and share it with the fellas since the majority of us were still under twenty-one. I probably would have taken a shot or two just to loosen up but I was the designated driver. You'd never catch me drinking and driving though. I wouldn't ever risk possibly taking someone's loved one away from them like how my dad was snatched away from me. My mama would kill me if I were to do that. That's if I wasn't already dead from the accident.

We were still at the bar getting shots when we noticed the group of cheerleaders who invited us to the party along with a few of their friends that I didn't recognize. They were probably new students. I was in the middle of talking to Troy about possibly leaving soon because we had class early tomorrow morning when I suddenly felt like someone was staring at me. I scanned the room and I was about to dip back into the conversation I was having with Troy when I did catch someone staring at me. Usually a chick would look away once she gets caught staring but this girl's eyes stayed glued on me. I was immediately captivated with her green eyes and caramel skin-tone. She looked exotic and definitely had my attention. Her intense stare had me more intrigued than I'd like to admit so I had to break away as if her beauty didn't faze me. Troy noticed her and swore up and down that she was staring at him and not me.

"Dude she's so damn fine! I caught her peeking at me on the low. You wouldn't know what to do with that anyway." He rubbed his hands together in anticipation again.

“Don't play yourself. She been looking at me the entire time and didn't so much glance towards you”, I claimed with my hands in my pockets.

“You must be Ray Charles or something because she was clearly staring at me fool.”

“Naw, I think you had one too many shots and it must have your vision blurry”, I proclaimed.

We were still jokingly going back and forth when the DJ decided to switch the pace of music from upbeat to a slow jam for the ladies as he put it. I was clowning Troy when she approached us and made me forget my train of thought. She looked even better up close. She had on a one piece jumpsuit that hugged all her curves but left something to the imagination. Her hair was styled in a bun which happened to be my favorite hairstyles on women for some reason. I glanced over at Troy and he was damn near foaming at the mouth. I'm pretty sure I looked calm and collected on the outside but on the inside my nerves were all over the place. I was hoping that my nervousness wouldn't permit me to say something stupid that turned her off because she looked like the type who always had other options, but I knew she was feeling me because if she wasn't she wouldn't have approached me. She leaned in towards my ear since the music was loud and I got a whiff of her perfume. It was light but reminded me of flowers and fruit. She had a hint of an accent when she spoke and it turned me on.

“It's Tristan right?”

“Yeah, that's my name. Who wants to know?”

“I want to know.”

I didn't resist when she grabbed me by the hand. I thought she was going to lead me to the dance floor where everyone else was, but instead she led me to the corner of the club where it was mostly isolated from the crowd. She took control and gently pushed me up against the wall then turned her back towards me. I could see Troy and the fellas egging me on in the distance as they danced with a few of the cheerleaders themselves. At first I was hesitant because I was contemplating on whether or not I should really be touching her even though she was all over me. I had conditioned myself to turn off my sexual desires over the years and be respectful, but the way she was grinding on me had me thinking otherwise. My mind didn't think twice when my hands dropped down to her hips, gripped them and pulled her closer to me. It was like second nature.

The DJ switched the song to Ciara’s “Body Party” record. I didn't really care for the song, but this song mixed with the liquor had the inner stripper bursting out of these chicks. I was enjoying my own personal lap dance from this womanly new drug that I had already found myself addicted to. The way she was moving her body had me in a trance and she didn't object when my hands started roaming her body. I felt myself getting excited when she wrapped her arms around my neck and continued grinding on my dick and I knew she felt it. I was in the zone until one of her friends approached us and killed our vibe.

"Girl, you need to do something about yo girl Jessica. She's in the bathroom throwing up everything in her stomach and I just can't." She animatedly gestured her hands as she spoke because she was just as drunk.

She rubbed her hands down my chest and walked away without even telling me her name and like a dog begging for a treat, I was hot on her trail. I lost sight of her in the crowd because everyone was leaving. When I reconnected with Troy and the squad all of these niggas were drunk. I was still looking for her as we left the club but I had to make sure Troy made it safely to my car because he definitely overdid it with the liquor. He'll regret it in the morning. I was about to give up hope when I noticed her helping her girl in a car. I probably looked overly anxious to get at her but I said fuck it.

I'm the go big or go home type of dude and she was finest thing I'd seen in a long time.

“So you know my name but I don't know yours, what's up with that?” I asked as I leaned on the side of her car with my hands in my pockets.

“You'll know it soon enough Tristan.”

“Damn, so that's how you gonna do me?”

“Don't you got a girl you should be chasing after?” She knew she had my full attention.

“If I had a girl I wouldn't even give you the time of day so what's up? Can I get yo number?” I was trying to spit game at her without seeming desperate.

“I'm a little busy babysitting my girls right now, but I'll be seeing you around campus.”

“I'm babysitting too so what does that mean?”

I stepped in closer to her to let her know what’s up. I was persistent when it came to the things I wanted. I always got what I wanted and she was the next top priority on my list. I had always been intrigued with a challenge.

“It means I can't give you my undivided attention right now because I'm busy, so I'll see you around campus. Drive safe." She opened the driver's door of her car and hopped in.

"Alright, I'll reconnect with you later."

I was trying to be cool about it but I wanted her bad. I couldn't stop thinking about her even after she pulled off. I made sure everyone got to their dorms safely when we made it back to campus which was no easy task considering everyone was sloppy drunk. I ended up having to carry a few people to their dorms. Troy was knocked out as I tried to carry him to our dorm. He woke up out of his drunken slumber a few times to throw up in the toilet since he couldn't make it to his room and he actually ended up falling asleep on the bathroom floor. I hope he can make it to class tomorrow because our coach didn't tolerate us missing class. It probably wasn't a good idea to go to a club on a Sunday night but who could pass up an invitation from some fine ass cheerleaders? I took a shower with Troy knocked out on the floor next to the toilet because I'd be damned if I had to carry another body. I was already tired from carrying everyone else. I slid into my bed and practically melted. My bed was so comfortable that it should have been a crime to ever abandon it. I started thinking about this exotic mystery chick that had been stealing space in my memory bank ever since I laid my eyes on her. I wanted to know everything about her and what made her so captivating but first I needed to know if she was single. Just because she gave me a lap dance didn't mean she wasn't already accounted for. A beautiful woman like that was usually already taken. I wanted to know her beyond her outward appearance but if she wasn't intelligent I knew I wouldn't be able to vibe with her. If she didn't have a sense a humor then I definitely wouldn't be able to be myself around her and if she wasn't humble and down to earth then I definitely couldn't bring her home to meet my family. I know that there's a stigma about men not having standards, but that's not necessarily true. For the most part, we all have standards and expectations. It's just a matter of whether you'll lower your standards or wait until you find someone who can meet your expectations and standards. That's where a lot of dudes just say fuck it and lower their standards.

The next morning I woke up refreshed with a smile on my face. I was still lying in bed since I had woke up early enough and had some extra time to just lounge around before getting ready for this introductory psychology class. I had a dream about little miss mysterious chick since she'd been really active in my subconscious ever since we met. I rolled over to take my phone off the charger and noticed that there was a huge wet spot in my bed.

What the fuck? I hadn't had a wet dream since middle school, but then again sex wasn't even on my radar in high school since I was so focused on more important things. I crawled out of bed and bundled my sheets together to throw them in the washing machine. After I threw my sheets in the washer, I went to the bathroom to check on Troy. This man was still knocked out by the toilet with dried vomit on the side of his mouth and his dreads sprawled everywhere. I tried to wake him up, but he was dead to the world. I washed my face and brushed my teeth because I had class in about 20 minutes.

I put on a basic t-shirt and basketball shorts since it was hot as hell outside. Plus, I didn't feel like getting dressed anyway. I walked out of our dorms and headed towards my class building. I ended up being a few minutes early so I just enjoyed my music until our instructor arrived. I was bobbing my head to some Chief Keef when she strolled into class in a gray sundress that made her look so elegant and angel like. She had her hair in another bun and I couldn't stop staring at her. She glanced at me and smiled when she caught me staring. I tried to quickly divert my attention elsewhere as if I wasn't just mentally undressing her. Our instructor finally showed up and I couldn't even pay attention the entire class. I was too busy fantasizing about all of the different positions I could bend her in. I had to calm down because I felt myself getting aroused. I was zoned out when the teacher snatched me out of fantasyland.

"Did you hear my question Mr. Smith?" He cleared his throat and pushed his glasses up with his index finger.

"Um, no sorry I didn't catch it. What was your question again?" I was one of those students who hated answering the question incorrectly in front of the class. I couldn't be perceived as if I didn't know anything.

"We are currently in chapter one and going over the basics of psychology, so knowing the basic terms is imperative to understanding what we're going to learn in this course. I asked if you know the basic term of psychology."

"The basic term is the study of human behavior", I answered without having to critically think.

This was too easy considering that my mama is a psychologist. I learned that shit in elementary thanks to her. This course was going to be an easy A. My eyes instantly zoomed in on my new crush to see what she was up to. She was busy taking notes and not really paying attention to my interaction with the instructor. The rest of the class flew by after that. I gathered my belongings and headed to the library to get that book we needed for class and since Troy didn't show up, I figured I'll grab his book too while I was at it. I went to the receptionist when I entered the building because I didn't want to be all day looking for these books. She pointed me to the aisle where the book was located and there she was again in the same aisle as me looking for the book. She was flipping through the pages of a book when she looked over at me and smiled again. I was nervous because I didn't know what to say to her. What do you say to a beautiful woman that's well put together?

“Now you have my undivided attention.” She smiled again and my palms started sweating.

“So you gone finally tell me your name or what?” I put my hands in my pockets. I had a bad habit of doing that when I was nervous.

“My name is Noel.”

“You got a bit of an accent. Where are you from?”

“I'm from the Virgin Islands. You ask a lot of questions.”

“How else are you going to learn new things if you don't ask questions?”

"Touché. Intelligence is the sexiest thing a man could ever wear and I can tell that you wear it well", she smiled.

"Do you tell that to your boyfriend too?" I confidently asked.

"Nice try, but no I don't have a boyfriend. I am very much single." She gave me the green light to go further with her.

"So you shouldn't have a problem with giving such an intelligent man like myself your number."

"You didn't check your pockets after the party last night?" Her eyebrows crinkled and it was the cutest thing ever.

"No, was there a reason I should have?"

"I wrote my number down and slipped it in your back pocket last night."

"I didn't even notice that. I'm glad you told me because I rarely check my pants pockets."

"Feel free to call me when you get it. I'll see you around."

She grabbed the books she needed and walked away. I was looking forward to getting to know her better. I smiled the entire way back to the dorms. I took out my house keys and entered our apartment. Troy was curled up on the couch with dark shades masking his eyes. I had to laugh because I already knew he was going to regret going so hard with liquor last night.

“I'm never drinking again”, he whined.

“Didn't nobody tell you take all those shots. I told you that you'll regret it in the morning.”

“Shut up man. I feel like somebody is knocking me upside my head with a fucking hammer. My shit is pounding.” He complained as he massaged his temple.

“What's up with the shades nigga?”

“It's sunny as hell outside and it's making my headache worst.”

“You'll be alright. You just gotta eat something to counter the liquor but guess what though?”

“What?”

“Remember the girl I danced with last night?”

“Yeah, I remember her fine ass.”

“I got her number and she's in our psychology class so now who can't handle what?” I asked like I had just won a victory.

“You still can't handle that. Does she know you're still a virgin?”

“Of course she doesn't because my swag is something serious. You would only know that if I told you.”

“Then you still can't handle that nigga. Most girls prefer a dude that's experienced if you know what I mean.”

“And some girls prefer a virgin over a nigga that’s had a hundred sex partners. Just because you're ““experienced”” by your definition doesn't mean you know what fuck you doing either.”

“Yeah, I guess you got a point since you put it that way. So what did I miss in class?”

“You didn't miss much. This class is gonna be an easy A.”

“Now that's what I like to hear. You plan on going back home because I need to make a trip to the Mil soon?”

“I’ll probably drive back next weekend to check on moms. Why, what's up?”

“Moms is having surgery sometime this week. She's making it seem like it's no big deal but I still want to check on her.”

"Oh, we can drive back then. I want to check on Destiny anyway."

"Okay cool."

After we chopped it up, we went to the Johnson Center to lift weights and put some shots up in the gym. I was currently in the weight room bench pressing to get my weight up for the season when I noticed Noel on a *StairMaster* machine. She looked good even while she was sweating. I wanted to stop what I was doing and approach her but I figured I had already been doing most of the chasing so if she wanted to talk to me she would have to approach me this time. I continued lifting weights. When she finished her workout, gathered her things and made her way towards me.

"So how much are you bench pressing?" she flirted.

"I'm at about 180 right now", I said proudly.

"So you shouldn't have a problem with lifting me huh?" She shifted her weight from one leg to the other and I couldn't help but notice her shapely hips.

"Girl I would lift you with ease and however you wanted me to." I flirted back and licked my lips. I hated that every time I was around her my mind instantly went to the gutter. She was the only one who had that effect on me.

“Maybe one day I'll be the judge of that”, she smiled at me.

“Yeah, maybe one day we can make that happen, but you have to earn that though”, I smiled from ear to ear.

“That's even better because I love a challenge. I'll see you around.”

She was about to walk away until she dropped her purse and the contents fell out. I bent down to help her pick up her things. I picked up her school I.D and looked at her picture. Her picture looked a lot better than mine but I also read her full name. It was Noel Watts. I lost my train of thought when her skin brushed up against mine in the process of me picking up her items. She smiled at me again and it was like she put a spell on me. I’d never been so captivated in my life and I could see myself potentially falling in love with her. I was starting to feel a bit whipped already and I barely even knew her. She wrapped her purse around her shoulder and stared at me for a while until she broke the intense silence between us. Man, if she only knew what I was thinking right about now.

“We should go out sometime”, she finally spoke up.

“I'm cool with that. I'll call you when I leave here to set something up”, I smirked.

“Don't forget either. I was expecting a call from you last night too, but that obviously didn't happen”, she smiled

“My bad. I was busy and I totally forgot. I'm not that inconsiderate, you'll see.”

“Well that's too bad. I had the impression that I'll be someone that you'll never forget about.”

“Well only time will tell for that one, but so far you are unforgettable”, I admitted.

“I thought so, and I can say the same about you. So I'll talk to you later?”

“Yeah, I'm not going to forget this time so you can look forward to it.”

She leaned in to give me a hug and I didn't resist a chance to have my body next to hers again. Even though she was clearly sweaty from her workout, she still had that light flowery scent lingering on her. My hands instantly draped down to her ass and she didn't protest when they lingered there longer than they should have. I couldn't help it. She was blessed with a nice ass. She laughed at me when our bodies finally disconnected and walked away with my eyes glued on her ass. I reconnected with Troy who was in the gym shooting around and told him about my interaction with Noel. He was hating a little bit because he was hoping that she was feeling him instead of me, but he already had chicks who he talked to so he shouldn't have felt some type of way.

I hopped in the shower as soon as we made it back to our dorms. I went through my pants pockets to find her number then saved it in my phone. I made myself comfortable in my room and jumped in my bed since it was definitely calling my name. I pulled my phone out again and waited for her to answer. She picked up on the third ring.

“Hey stranger.”

“I think I'm passed the stranger phase, don't you?”

“I don't know. I'm still figuring that out”, she flirted.

“Was I a stranger when you gave me that lap dance the other night?

“Yeah, you were. Just a fine stranger that I found appealing.”

“And here I was thinking that I was something special”, I laughed.

“You are special. I never give anyone a sample of one of the many things that I have to offer, so you should feel special.”

“So what made you move here to the states?” I was curious.

“My parents wanted a better life for me. Enough about me though. How was your last relationship?”

“I’ve never been in a relationship. I mean I talked to a few people here and there but it was never anything serious.”

“It seems like you're an all work and no play type of person.”

“I just like making sure that my business is getting handled first so relationships were never really my first priority.”

“I can tell that you're well-disciplined and controlled. Are you a virgin?”

“Damn is it that obvious?” I asked with disappointment dripping from my voice.

“It's probably not obvious to other women, but I have the ability of picking up on a person's mannerisms so it was easy for me to notice that about you. There’s innocence about you.”

“Is that a bad thing?” I was hoping she would say no because if not, my ego would have taken a punch.

“No I actually find it to be sexy and rare.”

“Well I'm glad to hear that.” I was about to flirt back with her until Troy busted in my room and interrupted my vibe.

“Nigga stop caking and come get yo ass busted in 2K real quick”, he demanded with a big ass bowl of cereal in his hands.

“Nigga stop hating and let me finish my conversation first.”

“You just saw her like five minutes ago. You sprung already! What a shame”, he joked with me as he continued to stuff his mouth.

“Shut up and go set up the game. I'll be in there to bust yo ass in minute.”

“Aye ask her if she got a sister that look just like her.”

“If she did have a sister, she probably wouldn't want a nigga looking like a Predator with them damn dreads all over the place. Now get out my room and mind yo business.” I threw one of my pillows at him so he can get the point.

“She liked me first anyway. Don’t be all day scrub.” He closed the door behind him and I turned my attention back to Noel.

“I gotta go, but I'm looking forward to getting to know you better”, I smiled.

“Same here. I got a feeling that this is only the beginning.”

40376995R00178

Made in the USA
Middletown, DE
10 February 2017